THE QUANTUM DRAGONSLAYER

THE QUANTUM DRAGONSLAYER, BOOK 1

KEVIN MCLAUGHLIN

ROLE OF THE HERO PUBLISHING COMPANY

Special thanks to Norma, whose keen eye made this book so much better!

ONE

Scott Free stared out the window of his spaceship at the dot that was Earth — and also at the other dot that wasn't supposed to be there.

It wasn't like him to worry. His approach to life was usually a carefree, "hakuna matata" style. But it was difficult not to feel a little concern when precisely nothing was going the way it was supposed to and he was fast running out of time.

"This is Stargazer One to Earth. Anyone out there hear me?" Scott called into his radio. He flipped through various frequencies, trying one after another. "Anyone at all? What the hell, people?"

Nobody was picking up. By itself, that was something of a concern. Scott had been away a much longer time than he'd originally intended, so long that it was possible radios had been discarded in favor of some new technology. Even if that had happened, though, he figured someone would still be listening to the airwaves somewhere on the planet.

But he was still decelerating so hard that the doppler effect could be screwing with his signal. Someone on Earth might well be receiving his call and only hearing static. Once he was down to a more reasonable speed, perhaps they'd hear him better.

No, the bigger concern was literally bigger. Like, planet-sized. Like, a new planet sitting there where there hadn't been one before.

Scott had almost thought he was off course when his ship zipped back into the solar system and saw he was making for a rendezvous with the fourth planet instead of the third. That was baffling enough. The autopilot had gone on the fritz more than once over the last two years, but it ought to at least be able to tell one planet from another!

When he realized the fourth planet was actually Earth, Scott stopped, blinking a few times.

"One, two, three... Three planets and then Earth. I see Mercury, Venus — and what the hell is that doing there?" he asked.

"Ruff," Toby replied.

"Thanks for the sage advice," Scott groused.

Not like he was expecting a lot more from the robot pup. Toby was capable of some limited conversation, albeit at a level only slightly more advanced than the Siri on his iPhone. But when the robot dog didn't have a good answer, he tended to drop into acting less like an assistive intelligence and more like a dog.

"No need to get sarcastic," Toby replied.

"Yeah, there was. But never mind. I suppose we'll see soon enough."

Someone on Earth would know what was going on. Scott wished he'd thought to have a telescope aimed back at Earth so that he could watch his home while he was away on the trip. The whole idea of letting the changes be a surprise present to enjoy was sounding a lot less fun now that he was finally opening the gift.

A new planet didn't just appear out of nowhere. It wasn't one of the other eight planets, either. They were all more or less where they were supposed to be. Scott checked the orbits of every planet in the system by his logs. They were all slightly off. Like, Venus was a bit further out from the sun than it should have been. Earth was just a shade closer. Pluto's orbit was way more erratic than it used to be. He'd barely been able to find the little planetoid, it had swung out so far from the sun.

The only thing Scott could think of was that this new world was a rogue planet, picked up by the sun as it journeyed through space. The planet probably came close enough to get dragged in, jostled all the other orbits a tad on the way in, and then settled into what looked like a stable orbit.

He almost changed course to check out the new world. What an exciting bit of exploration that would be! Scott could end up being the first human to walk on a new world. That would be one for the books for sure.

Regretfully, he decided to pursue prudence this time. His ship wasn't designed to go checking out new planets, and Scott wasn't confident about his ability to get back home again if he went wandering. The ship might be able to take off again after he landed, but it might not. The idea of exploring a new planet sounded fun. The thought of being stuck there didn't.

Earth it would be. Scott settled in for the last leg of his journey, looking forward to being home among other people soon. Two years was a damned long time to be by himself.

"Although you've been good company," he told Toby.

"Thank you. I wish I could say the same, but the past

two years have been incredibly bad for my circuits," the robot dog replied.

"Are you kidding? This has been like a vacation!"

"Oh. So getting a hole punched in the side of the ship by a meteorite is your idea of a day at the beach?" Toby asked.

Well, no. That was besides the point, though. "OK, we have had a few rough patches—"

"Or when you went outside to repair the radar dish, dropped a wrench, and instead of coming back inside for another," Toby said, "you went after it and almost did a Dutchman."

That hadn't been his finest moment, either. Toby had said to forget it — he could always 3D print another wrench. But Scott hated wasting anything, and besides...

"It worked, though."

"Yes. How, I have no idea. Your continued breathing defies logic and probability," Toby said.

On that much, they agreed. Scott frowned, wondering how much longer he had before the ticking bomb in his head exploded.

Pretty soon he'd be able to see if this whole space gambit had been worth it or not. Scott sweated at the thought. It had to have been enough. A billion dollars spent on this mission couldn't just be a waste of money and time. No, soon he'd be back on an Earth that was technologically advanced enough to save him.

TWO

Scott's thoughts drifted back to the diagnosis. FFI — fatal familial insomnia — was a rare enough disease that his father had been diagnosed far too late to do anything but wave goodbye as his brain cells turned into mush. Bjorn Free had always been a driven man, given to working long hours and not sleeping much. No one had thought it odd that he was sleeping less and less, until he started having hallucinations about rabid poodles chasing him around the office building.

That got everyone's attention right away. He was shipped off to Mass General in restraints, sedated, and finally got the first sleep he'd had in almost two weeks. After what seemed like six million rounds of testing, the doctors had finally identified the problem. It was a little gene that was screwed up, telling his body to kick out a specific prion that wasn't supposed to be there.

Those prions were lodging in his brain and slowly killing neurons. The first symptoms involved sleeplessness. Then came the hallucinations. After that came memory loss, dementia, and eventually death.

Nobody had any clue what a cure would even look like. Prions weren't treatable, and a body producing lethal prions was a death sentence. It wasn't a matter of if the disease would kill its victim. It was just a matter of when, and managing symptoms until it happened.

Because it was a genetic disease, the doctors tested the rest of the family as well. Scott's mother Olivia was fine. Her genes were excellent, apparently. But the Free couple's son had the bad luck of inheriting his father's crappy genetics.

"Well, son, it seems like you take after your father! You've got that funny little PRPN gene, just like him," Doctor Obelin had said.

It was probably the nicest death sentence anyone had ever delivered.

"But we're catching it early, right? That means you can treat me?" Scott asked.

He had just come to his appointment from visiting his father at Chelsea Jewish, a nice old folks' home where he was slowly drooling and babbling himself to death. The idea of "a fate worse than death" had always seemed foolish to Scott. What could be worse than dying? Once you were dead, that was it. No more chances. No more skydiving or spearfishing off the coast of Australia. Dead was dead. Living was better.

Then he'd seen his father turn from a powerhouse of a business investor into a mindless lunatic in less than a year, and he had elected to revise his opinion on the subject. Some things really were worse than death.

For the first time since the whole ordeal with his father began, fear grabbed Scott by the throat. He cleared it with a cough, trying to banish the feeling without much success. Of course there would be a way to treat him.

"Well, we will help you manage symptoms, of course. And we recommend not having children. A vasectomy might be advisable," Obelin said. "You don't have any children yet, correct?"

"No, I don't have kids," Scott said. He was twenty-four. Plenty of time for children to slow him down when he was older. Then the implications of what the doctor was saying sank in. "Wait, are you saying you can't fix this?"

"Fix it?" the doctor asked, staring at Scott with a blank expression.

"Cure me. Make me better. Make this not happen to me," Scott explained, drawling out his words.

"No, son. I'm sorry. We can't cure prion diseases at all, and one where it's a faulty gene making your body produce the prions?" Obelin shook his head. "There's nothing we can do. In a hundred years, maybe we'll be able to solve problems like this. But not now."

Scott stormed off and went to get a second opinion. When the second opinion said the same thing, he sought out a third and a fourth and a fifth. He went to darned near every doctor he could find who knew anything about Fatal Familial Insomnia. It was a rare enough disorder that few doctors had treated patients with the disease, let alone studied it in a detailed manner.

The answer was always the same. No cure, no hope, set your affairs in order so that when the ticking time bomb inside you goes off and you turn into a demented, sleepless lunatic, you're well prepared.

Scott's father died the next year. He hadn't recognized any of his family members for months, so Scott was left wondering if he should mourn at his funeral or if he should have done so months prior.

He wasn't ready to walk down that road, and he wasn't

ever going to be. Everything he'd learned from the doctors kept coming back around to the same thing Obelin had said. Medicine was still too far out to solve the problem.

That was not an insolvable problem. Scott decided he would find a way to put off the disease until medicine had caught up with his needs.

THE CHIRP of an alarm brought Scott out of his musing. He checked the pilot's console in front of him. Earth was visible! He was almost home. Excited, he trained the ship's telescope down on the land below, but he was coming up on the side facing away from the sun, and nothing was really visible.

Scott frowned. Shouldn't there be city lights down there? He was fairly sure you could see Earth's cities from space at night. He tapped the send button on his radio and opened his mouth to speak. Now that he was close enough and moving slowly enough, surely they'd be able to pick up his transmission.

That was when he realized the beeping alarm hadn't been warning him that he was close to Earth. It was letting him know there was a big thing flying straight at him. Seeing the flashing words "COLLISION IMMINENT" on one's pilot console had a way of releasing enough adrenaline to push one into solving the crisis.

Scott flipped the telescope up in the direction of the object. Was it space junk? Maybe it was a ship, sent out to meet him?

No guess could prepare him for what he saw when the lens finally came into focus. He was staring straight into the eyes and very large teeth of what he could only call a dragon.

THREE

"**H**oly shit!"

What else could you say when a fifty-foot-long winged lizard was flying toward your spaceship? Scott felt like it was an entirely appropriate initial reaction.

His second thought was a healthy dose of skepticism. While a dragon wasn't the same thing as the pack of rabid poodles his father had started seeing when he became ill, it was if anything even more far-fetched. Was he starting to come down with symptoms already? The disease could strike at any time from early adulthood onward. That same old dread gripped Scott's heart. He was almost home. Was this the beginning of the end, when he was so close?

"Ruff," Toby agreed from beside him. Like Scott, the robot was staring out the big window on the front of the ship. The dragon was close enough that Scott could see it without the telescope now. It was getting bigger, too.

"Wait — do you see it too?" Scott asked.

"Big flying lizard?" Toby replied. Scott nodded. "Then yes."

Relief eased all the tension that had been building in Scott's belly. He exhaled hard and settled back against his chair. Thank god. If Toby saw the same thing he did, it couldn't possibly be a hallucination. He wasn't sick yet. There was still time for him to find a cure.

He sat bolt upright in his chair as the implications of those thoughts struck home. If the dragon wasn't a trick his brain was playing, then that meant...

Scott's eyes went wide as saucers. The thing was fast! It was almost on top of him, looming huge in the window. Its wings were outstretched like it was gliding, even though there wasn't any air. How the hell was it gliding in space? What was it breathing?

Scott grabbed the flight controls in front of him and jerked the stick sideways, trying to steer away from the dragon. Nothing happened. It was getting closer. Another few seconds and it would be on top of him, and the damned thing was almost as big as his ship!

He wiggled the control stick some more. Still no response.

"Autopilot?" Toby said softly.

"Oh," Scott replied. Right.

He flipped the switch, shutting down the autopilot. This time when he yanked the stick to the left, the planet whirled away beneath him. The effect made him feel dizzy.

Then the dragon slammed into the front of his spaceship with a resounding clang.

It clamped on with four legs, wings still spread out, tail whipping around wildly. The engines whined as Scott pushed the throttle up higher without any success. Somehow, the dragon was stopping his forward acceleration. It sank teeth into the ram scoop that made up the entire front of the Stargazer. Scott felt the crunching vibration of steel breaking apart through his seat.

It ripped a chunk of the ship away and spat it out. Then it bit down again.

"A dragon is eating my spaceship," Scott said, not quite able to believe what he was seeing despite the evidence.

The tail continued slashing around like a cat would while playing with prey. It sailed forward, striking the hull just below Scott's window. Then it swung away again and vanished into the ram scoop, where it slammed against metal hard enough to rock the entire ship before whipping back out toward him again. Back and forth it went while the dragon chewed chunks out of the scoop.

That ram scoop was what made an extended flight like his possible. It was charged with a mild current that allowed it to pick up particles as he sped through space. Those were then fed into the particle accelerator as fuel and ejected as photons to propel the ship through space. The result was a starship that refueled as it flew.

Clang. Chomp. Crunch. Chomp. The dragon continued bashing and chewing his very expensive ship into rubble. The tail slapped the hull next to his window. It was close enough that Scott ducked instinctively to avoid the blow. He slowly lifted his head back up again, eyeing the tail warily.

"Hey, you big lizard! Go find something else to eat! This ship cost me a lot of money!" Scott hollered at the thing.

It didn't act like it heard him. Which was probably a good thing, once he thought about it a little. Those teeth were very large, and Scott decided he preferred a dragon chewing on his ship to a dragon chewing on him.

It occurred to Scott that very soon those claws and teeth

were going to reach something vital, and either his ship would explode, or it would vent all his air into space. Either way, he wasn't going to survive the experience. It was time to do something about this unwelcome guest.

The whipping tail gave him an idea. A few taps on the computer let him access the settings of the ram scoop. Scott flipped off all the safeties and then opened the window that controlled the scoop's power setting. It was only putting out a very mild charge. But that could be tweaked.

The theory was that if the ship ever needed a lot of fuel quickly, it could fly through an upper atmosphere and turn the scoop's power up to maximum. That would yank in a ton more matter, refilling the reserve tanks quickly.

What would it do to a dragon's tail? Scott didn't know, but decided it was time to find out. He waited until the tail was once again vanishing into the scoop and then pressed the button.

The Stargazer shuddered. More alarms beeped. Red lights flashed all around him. Scott didn't even know what half of the alarms signals were for. Most of them had never turned on in the two years he'd been on board.

But the dragon was definitely pissed off. It stopped chewing his ship — a plus — and ground its forelimbs into the hull even more deeply. That part wasn't quite as reassuring. At least the tail had stopped whipping around. Scott had grown tired of worrying it would swing up just a little higher and strike his window.

"Wait, where is the tail now?" Scott asked.

"Ram scoop blocked," Toby replied, staring at his console.

Oh, that alarm on his left was flashing those words, wasn't it? The tail was in the scoop. The scoop was blocked. Those two things were probably not a coincidence.

"Warning, orbit decay," Toby said.

Scott looked to his right. Another red light was showing on an indicator that read precisely that. The ship's nose was slowly tilting back toward Earth, and the planet was rapidly growing larger in his window. He grabbed the control stick and struggled to correct his course, but although the engines screamed and put out enough thrust that they should have been flying away from the planet, it kept growing larger instead of smaller.

Somehow, the dragon was still pulling him down. Its wings were spread out; each was ribbed like the wings of a bat, and those ribs were shining, even glowing. He hadn't noticed it before with the sunlight in the background, but as they drew closer to the planet, the sun became eclipsed and the glow much more prominent.

"Glowing space dragons," Scott muttered. "Not how I expected to go out, but real glowing space dragons are better than imaginary rabid poodles, I suppose."

"Ruff," Toby agreed.

FOUR

Crashing was not part of the game plan. Landing the ship was going to be hard enough without a dragon attached to its nose. But despite everything he could think to try, the Stargazer was still falling toward Earth. It seemed like it was picking up speed, too.

"Toby, you got any ideas?" Scott asked. He was fresh out, or he never would have asked a glorified walking app for help.

"Playing "I Got Ideas" by Tony Martin," Toby replied, before beginning to croon a song that sounded like it was from the middle of the last century.

"Toby, stop it," Scott said.

The dog shut up. If he was going to have musical accompaniment for his demise, Scott thought it would be better to play something more appropriate. Something dangerous, with an edge.

"Toby, play some AC/DC," Scott said.

The song "Highway to Hell" started pounding from the robot's speaker system, the bass so strong it vibrated the ship. That was more like it. "Highway to Hell" felt more practical for the moment.

"OK, what have I got that I can work with?" Scott asked. "A ship, a dragon, a whole lot of junk in storage, um..."

He had a spear-gun back there, along with some other assorted stuff. Maybe he could get into a space-suit, grab the spear gun, crawl out there along the ship's hull, and kill the dragon?

Scott glanced back outside, where a maw big enough to swallow him whole was taking another bite from his ship. Wait — was it breathing fire now, too?

Maybe discretion was the better part of valor here.

Besides, with his luck he'd just fall off the ship instead of being eaten. It was a long way down either way, but the thought of being inside his ship felt better than the idea of floating down in just a suit.

Wind was visibly whipping past the dragon now, moving its wings. It held them open as best it could, but it was having a hard time keeping them outstretched. Did it think it could keep the whole ship aloft? Scott didn't think that was likely, given what little he knew of aerodynamics. The ship was bigger than the dragon. Not by much, but enough. It had to weigh a lot more, too.

He could see land down there. It was dark, but the moon was shining, sparkling off of the water and dimly illuminating the ground. Why wasn't he burning up, anyway? They were definitely low enough to be in the atmosphere, but the ship didn't even seem to be warming up. Either the dragon was acting as a heat shield, or it was slowing the Stargazer's descent.

The ship was low enough now that Scott could make out some specific details of the land below. There was a coastline and a massive body of water. It looked like maybe it was the east coast of North America, but he wasn't seeing the lights of any cities at all, so that couldn't be right. New York, DC, and other big urban areas would light up the night no matter what time it was. No, it had to be some other east coast.

"Just great. I don't speak anything but English. I hope whoever lives down there can, too. Hey, Toby, can you translate French?" Scott asked.

"*Oui, je peux traduire le français,*" Toby replied.

"I don't understand a word you just said," Scott said, staring at the dog.

"*C'est parce que vous êtes stupides et que je suis intelligent,*" Toby said.

Scott narrowed his eyes and glared at the robot. He might not know French, but the words *vous êtes stupides* had a familiar ring to them.

"Unless you want to become spare parts, watch the smart mouth," Scott said.

"Recommend taking crash precautions," Toby said.

Scott looked back out the window. The ground was significantly closer. Why, he could almost make out individual trees down there! Scale was difficult to tell from up that high, but they looked like really big trees.

Those trees were coming up fast. Oh, so fast.

Scott swallowed hard. Crash precautions, right. What were they again? His safety harness was already hooked up. The buckles were set. Scott checked each in turn to make sure. Fear was making his thoughts feel like molasses. What else did he have to do?

"Helmet," Toby said. The dog was sitting next to him on the floor.

"Right! Thanks," Scott said.

He snatched it up and set it atop his head. It locked down with the rest of his suit with an audible click. The hissing sound meant air was flowing properly, which would have been useful a little while ago when he was worried about the tail breaking his window.

"What about you?" Scott asked the dog.

"I'm clamped to the floor with magnets and made of metal. Worry about yourself, please," Toby replied.

"Being made of metal must be awfully nice at times like this."

"Oh, it is."

The altimeter said he was at a thousand feet. That meant the ground should be less than ten seconds away. Just a few breaths and he'd learn whether he was going to survive this wreck or not. Scott closed his eyes and started counting. He didn't need to see the ground rushing up to meet him. Bad enough to hear the steady rending noises the dragon was making as it continued tearing up his ship.

He'd reached twelve when the dragon let out an ear-piercing roar that made him open his eyes back up. It was still out there on the nose of his ship, wings furled out as far as they could go — but it was upside down, belly in toward the Stargazer, so Scott wasn't sure how much good the wings were doing, even if they were glowing twice as brightly as before.

The ship should've already crashed. The altimeter said four hundred feet, though. That was odd. It was still dropping, but nowhere near as fast as Scott thought it should have been. The fall was more like a slow drift downward. He could see the treetops beneath him clearly now in the reflected moonlight. They were so close it almost looked like he could jump out and land on them.

Only a few heartbeats later, the ship was close enough

that he really could've reached out to touch the tree limbs. They, in turn, reached out and touched his ship. A lot. The Stargazer tore through the upper canopy, shattering limbs and smashing entire trunks of a few unfortunate trees. The foliage was slowing his descent even more. Maybe he was going to survive this after all!

It was dark under the canopy. Still falling, Scott could barely see anything now, just the occasional flicker of wing-light glinting off leaves or branches as the ship continued smashing its way toward the ground.

Then it slammed to a stop with an earth-shuddering crash. Scott snapped forward against his restraints, which held him in place just fine. Unfortunately, the laptop he'd been working with earlier in the day was only secured by velcro on the counter behind him. The impact sent it flying forward. It cracked against the back of Scott's helmet.

He saw a brief flash of light, and then nothing.

FIVE

Dragoncon was a good time, and Scott attended every year he could. The year his father died, he almost skipped. The depression over losing his dad, coupled with the knowledge of his own impending horrible demise, was enough to leave Scott wanting to live the rest of his days as a couch potato re-watching episodes of 'Game of Thrones' on a big screen TV.

But he'd mustered up the energy to go, anyway. Luckily for him, too, because that event changed the entire course of his life.

Getting drunk seemed like the logical thing to do at a convention. Why not? His liver was going to outlast his brain no matter what he did to it. Plus, there was a cute girl hanging out at the bar whose eye he wanted to catch. Maybe she'd sit on the stool next to him? There were only a few empty ones left.

Instead, a big guy with a scruffy-looking face, jeans, and a t-shirt took the seat. Scott gave a deep sigh and rolled his eyes. His luck just wasn't ever going to change, was it?

The stranger leaned in and waved the bartender over.

"Sam Adams, please."

The guy behind the bar nodded, grabbed a bottle, popped the top off, and plunked it in front of him. Then he glanced at Scott. "You need anything?"

"Yeah, I'll have the same," Scott said. Didn't really matter what he drank. He was three beers in, so they all tasted about the same.

"Having fun at the con?" the guy next to him asked.

The bartender came back with another beer and plopped it on a cardboard coaster in front of Scott. He took a sip. Cold, just a little bitter, and a decent flavor — turned out you could taste the fourth beer after all.

"Yeah, I guess so," Scott replied.

"You guess so? Or you are?"

"Not super much," Scott replied. It was Friday, he'd just arrived, and the place was hopping. Tons of people in awesome costumes and more things to do or see than you could shake a stick at. But he just wasn't feeling it this year. He figured he could be excused for being a bit melancholy. At least he'd gotten off the sofa and shown up.

"What's bugging you?" the stranger asked.

Scott eyeballed him. "How do you know something's bugging me?"

"Because you're at one of the most fun events in the world and you look like someone ran over your dog."

"My dad just died," Scott admitted.

"Oh. Man, that sucks. I'm sorry," the guy replied. "Hey, I'm Michael Anderle."

Scott stared at him blankly.

"Michael Anderle. I write books. Um, Kurtherian... You know what? Never mind," Michael said, smiling broadly. "It doesn't really matter."

"If you say so," Scott replied, liking the guy's easy

manner despite the rough introduction. "I'm Scott. Scott Free."

Michael's eyebrows shot up. "Really?"

Scott leaned back and gave an exaggerated sigh. "Yes, really. My parents were suckers for a pun. So were my paternal grandparents. My dad's name was Bjorn."

It took a moment, but then Michael got it. He chuckled.

"My mom was just as bad, although that was really more luck than anything else," Scott said. "Her name was Olivia."

It was Michael's turn to give Scott a blank look.

"Olivia Free," Scott said. "Her nickname was Liv."

This time Michael laughed, a big rolling sound that was infectious enough to bring a smile to Scott's lips. He found himself laughing as well. Maybe it was the beer, or maybe this guy was just good company, but he felt better than he had in a long time.

"That isn't my only problem, though," Scott said, the words spilling out before he had time to think them over.

"No?"

Scott suddenly realized he was on the verge of giving away much more personal information than he'd been planning to share. Did he really want a random stranger knowing about the time bomb ticking away inside his brain? Maybe he could couch the problem in a way that sounded generic?

"Suppose a guy had an illness that science couldn't cure. The doctors said it would be a hundred years or more before they could fix it, and he was going to die a horrible death. What do you think he should do?" Scott asked.

"This is for a book?" Michael asked. "You're a writer?"

Aha! Yes, that would do as an alibi. "It's a story idea that I'm thinking of, yeah."

"Well, for science fiction, the guy could just freeze himself, maybe. He could go into suspended animation, or stasis, then wake up a century later to be cured," Michael said.

"Can we do that right now? I didn't think that sort of tech existed."

Michael's face fell, his brows knitted together. "No, we don't. The story is near-future, then?"

"Yeah."

"What about time dilation?" a voice over Scott's other shoulder asked. Another man was standing there. He flashed a smile. "Sorry, I couldn't help but overhear the conversation, and it sounded interesting. I'm—"

"What's time dilation?" Scott asked.

"Relativity. When something goes fast, it basically slows down in relation to the rest of the universe," Michael said. "Yeah, that might work for your story."

"So if someone just got into a fast jet, more time would pass for the rest of the world than did for them?" Scott asked. That didn't sound right to him at all. He'd been on plenty of planes, and didn't feel a day younger than he should be.

"No!" Michael laughed. "We're talking about really fast speeds, if you want to see a visible difference."

"Yeah," the other man said. "Like, a significant percentage of the speed of light. Over 99 percent to see really serious changes. You can have hundreds of years pass for each year of the traveler, then. By the way, great to meet you, Michael! I'm David Alastair Hayden."

"Nice to meet you, too," Michael said.

The two men shook hands across the bar in front of Scott, who was leaning back in his chair, deep in thought. It didn't sound like either of those ideas were incredibly practical, but the high-speed one sounded more interesting than the idea of becoming a popsicle.

"How would one get to 99 percent of the speed of light?" Scott asked.

"Right now? You can't," Michael said.

"Oh, I don't know about that. There's some interesting research being done on photon rockets right now," David said.

"What's that?" Scott asked, jumping on any thread of hope in the conversation.

"It's a rocket that uses a particle accelerator to smash atoms into photons, and then drive the ship forward using the photons," David said. "In theory, we might be able to reach 99.9999 percent of light speed using that sort of drive."

"Wow, that's pretty interesting," Michael said.

"Yeah, saw the article in *Acta Astronautica*. It's still early stages of looking into this sort of thing, but it sounds like it might have serious promise down the road," David replied.

The two continued their conversation around Scott, almost oblivious to him now that he'd stopped speaking. He was more interested in planning. Photon rockets could boost him to enough speed that he could live on a ship for a year or two and then return to an Earth where hundreds of years had gone by. It was the answer to all of his problems.

So what if the technology didn't exist yet? Bjorn Free had died an exceptionally wealthy man and left everything to his wife and son. Scott had more money than he knew what to do with — until that moment, anyway. Now he knew precisely what he would do with his father's billions.

Scott was going to use the money his father left him to save himself from his father's disease.

SIX

Thunder had rocked the sky during the dark hours of the morning just before the sun rose. Tamara had remained in her people's shelter, huddled there with the rest, wondering if the world was truly coming to an end.

It hadn't, of course. Dawn broke over the land like it did every other day. Whatever the noise, light, and thunder had been, it went away. But it left her curious. What had it been? What did it mean for her people? Was it a danger or an opportunity?

She took two of her friends out to seek answers at first light. They walked alongside her, silent and lost in their own thoughts. It was risky to be out and about during the day, but the forest was thick enough that they were mostly invisible from the air. There would be plenty of time to spot an incoming dragon and shelter themselves out of view.

Tamara motioned for Kendall to take point. They used wordless hand motions to pass messages back and forth. Better to be unheard as well as unseen as they slipped quietly through the brush. If they were lucky, they might stumble across a deer during the journey. Food for the hearth was always a welcome thing.

Piper trailed alongside her. She exchanged a glance with the other woman. Her friend's eyes held the same glimmer of fear mixed with excitement that Tamara's own must have shown. That they were headed toward something momentous was undoubtable. Whatever had made all the noise had struck the ground only a few miles away. Close enough to be an easy walk. Far enough to let their trepidation rise as they journeyed forth.

Tamara heard wingbeats overhead twice on their walk. Each time, she made the signal to be still, and her friends froze in place. The dragons were growing more numerous as each year passed. How long would it be before they found her people and dug them out of the warren where they hid? Some days if felt like each dawn was a gift that might be taken away at any moment.

Kendall paused at a ridge and motioned her forward. Tamara slipped up as silently as she could, crouching close to the ground beside her friend. What she saw in the small valley below was difficult to describe.

It looked something like one of the structures from the Old World. But where those were rusted, twisted, half-burned ruins, this one looked intact. Had all the old frames once fallen from the sky? That didn't match the stories her people told. The old ones said that once, humans had lived in the dead cities, before the dragons came.

Younger minds scoffed at the idea. There had always been dragons for as long as any living person could recall. The idea of a time before the dragons when humans wandered freely over the world was ridiculous. And yet, Tamara was a hunter, free to roam the world and explore while seeking supplies for her people. She had been to those ruined places. She'd seen the remnants of the cities. They did indeed look like they had been inhabited by humans, so there had to be something to the old tales.

Tamara tried to imagine a world where people lived above the ground in massive structures like the one before her. It was hard to picture what that might have looked like.

Piper came up beside her and leaned in, pointing below. She leaned in close to Tamara to whisper at her. "Look at that."

It was hard to see what she was talking about at first, but then Tamara spotted the flash of iridescent green hidden amidst the brush. Was it a dragon? She tensed, ready to flee if the thing came after them.

But the dragon wasn't moving. If it was indeed a dragon, it was either sleeping or dead.

The latter was unlikely, but incredibly dangerous. Oh, there had been a few dragons that had died, but they always came to claim their own when they fell to age or illness. Tamara knew to avoid their corpses because they were certain to draw more dragons in time.

"It's dead, and half buried under the metal structure," Piper said. Her eyes were the keenest of the trio. "Did the building fall on it?"

It was plausible. But if this structure had fallen from the sky and slain a dragon, could it be used to kill more? Would more buildings fall down, perhaps on top of her home? The metal tower was new and frightening to Tamara, but her people were depending on her to ferret out its secrets.

"We need to know more," Tamara said.

"It might be dangerous," Kendall replied. He looked nervous at the idea of going down.

"We are warriors of Hero's Keep. We fear nothing," Tamara said.

She felt like her words were as much to convince herself as Kendall. Tamara wanted the same thing he did — to flee this place and leave its mysteries behind her, yet a burning curiosity filled her at the same time. More than ever, she felt like the gains might well be worth the risk involved.

"Quietly, follow me," Tamara said.

They slipped down the hillside in a single file. Tamara gripped her spear tightly, holding it at the ready as she snuck toward the tower. The dragon was more visible from this closer vantage point. It was indeed dead, only the head and a few other parts extending out from beneath the tower. She burned with the need to know how it had happened, to discover the secrets behind this place. For the first time in a long while, she felt the flickering of hope that she might be on the verge of discovering something to save her people.

They needed that more than ever. Time was running out for Hero's Keep. Surrounded by enemies and dragons, it was only a matter of moons until a war broke out that no one was going to win.

That structure held the key to a different path. She felt sure of it. The smooth sides of the tower spoke to the power of whoever had built it. This was no crudely hacked together tool. The tower looked like the ancient buildings in the cities, but new and fresh. Who could tell what treasures it might contain?

"Be ready for anything," she whispered to Piper, who nodded in reply.

Her hunting party closed in on the base of the tower warily. Danger was everywhere. Death came on swift wings. But with luck, she might come away from this place with tools that would turn the tide in favor of her Keep.

SEVEN

"You really should be getting up now," Toby's voice came to Scott as if from far away.

Scott groaned and opened his eyes a crack. He snapped them closed again, wanting more than anything to slip back into unconsciousness. His head was pounding, and his entire body felt like it had been beaten with a hammer. Worst, he was dangling chest-down from his harness.

Dangling hurt, but not enough to knock him out again. Just enough to be incredibly uncomfortable, damn it. He groaned again, more theatrically this time, and opened his eyes again.

The first thing he saw was the dragon's head leering at him from the ground outside. Scott jerked completely awake, struggling at his straps. The thing hadn't eaten him yet. Maybe he still had time to get away!

But it wasn't moving.

Scott realized it was still. Totally, completely motionless. The dragon's eyes were open, but they didn't seem to be staring at anything in particular. His eyes traced the line of its neck away from those terrible teeth, down its throat toward the body...

Nope, no body. The neck ended abruptly at the edge of his ram scoop, which had driven itself a couple of feet into the ground. Red blood was splashed about on the ground from the severed neck. That dragon looked dead as a door nail.

"Well, I'll be damned," he said. "Scott Free, dragonslayer."

He liked the sound of that. Although he hoped it wasn't some sort of protected species or someone's escaped pet. He was hundreds of years in the future. Who knew what sort of things the people of this time did? The dragon had to have been engineered in a lab. Some sort of Jurassic Park type thing, maybe. Scott was pretty sure that self-defense was a legitimate reason for killing a dragon. Hopefully, whatever legal system this new world used would agree.

The Stargazer was pretty beaten up. Dragon chomps aside, crashing through the trees hadn't been good for the ship, and if the impact with the ground wasn't as hard as he'd been expecting, he'd still struck hard enough to sever a dragon's head from its body. That couldn't have been good for the ship, either.

Scott unbuckled his straps carefully. The window was about six feet below him, cracks running all through it. If he tumbled forward out of his chair and smacked into the window, he wasn't sure it would hold. The ground was a long way down out there.

Amazingly, the ship still had power. Scott flipped on a few switches. The radio still worked, the lighting was still active, and he even had power for the hatches and ventilation. The advantages of having a fusion reactor in the core of the vessel. He could run that thing for a long time on low power.

Once the straps of his harness were undone, Scott swung over to rest his feet on the side of the pilot's console. He stretched, feeling every bruise the fall had left on his body. His headache didn't seem to be fading, either.

"Toby, what are we going to do now?"

"Primary mission imperative: find a cure for Fatal Familial Insomnia. We are currently 3,033 miles from your destination," Toby replied. "Recommend finding transportation."

The destination was how far away? U Cal Berkeley was where they had developed the cure for his illness, or so the last radio message he'd received had said. That was over a year ago. It had taken Scott a long time to get the ship back home, even moving at almost the speed of light.

Scott tried the radio again. "Stargazer One to anyone out there. Mayday. Crash landed. Need assistance. Anyone?"

There wasn't any reply. Scott waited a little while and then tried again with the same results. Was there no one listening to radio broadcasts anymore? Scott supposed that was possible, but it felt weird. That was one tech he'd figured would last pretty much forever.

"Well, I guess we ought to go see if we can find some people. Get some help," Scott said.

"Woof," Toby replied, nodding his head vigorously.

The climb up to the hatch was a pain, literally. Scott's chest was a web-work of bruises. The harness had saved his life, but everything they said about falls was true. It really was the sudden stop at the end that hurt the most.

He considered climbing back into the hold to grab some gear. There was still plenty of food on board the ship. He had water and a bunch of other supplies. The Stargazer was well-stocked. Scott had even thought to pack a bunch of interesting curios, things he thought might sell for something once he was in the future. Just in case the extensive investment portfolio he'd left behind was lost. He had a small stash of gold as well, which would likely still be transferrable into currency even in the far future. One could never be too careful, and gold had been a staple for a long time.

But it was a long climb up into the crew area and the hold. They were in the middle section of the ship, which was now up from where he was, thanks to the nose stabbing into the ground. He decided he was too tired and hurt too much to bother. Coming back for the rest of his supplies later made more sense.

Scott laid his hand against the panel beside the hatch. It bleeped, and then flashed red. He stared at the device, wondering why it wasn't working. He placed his palm against the reader again, and got the same result. It took a third failure before Scott realized he was still wearing the gloves for his suit.

"Of course that's not going to work," he said, and slid the gloves off one at a time. He dropped them down toward the seat, where they clattered into place next to his discarded helmet. The rest of the suit really ought to go as well, but it could wait until he was outside.

This time the palm reader flashed green. The hatch growled at him and then rolled open. Scott pulled himself up into the airlock. A second panel rested on the wall a few feet away. When he pressed his hand to that, the door behind him slid shut. There was the briefest of pauses as air hissed into the chamber, but it didn't take the airlock long to figure out there was atmosphere outside. The outer door opened up.

Scott's first impression was to gag. He almost put his hand on the panel again to shut the door, the smell was so bad. It was like old meat and rotting vegetables stirred together. The heat that rolled in with the air was intense enough that he broke immediately into a sweat.

"Holy shit, it's hot out there." He wondered again just where he'd landed. The whole crashing-with-a-dragon-eating-his-ship thing had distracted him from being able to take proper coordinate readings on his way in, and the ship's GPS was totally borked. It wasn't giving him any location at all.

He wasn't going to figure it out by sitting in his ship, though. Scott crawled out through the hatch and grabbed a handhold on the outer hull. A ladder ran down the entire length of the ship, from the tip of the scoop to the tail of the engine. Being careful not to slip — the ground was a long way down, and his fingers were already greasy with sweat — Scott began lowering himself hand over hand toward the ground.

Toby's head popped out of the hatch. "Do you require assistance?"

"No, I've got this," Scott replied. But how was Toby going to get down? He didn't have hands to grab the rungs. While he was trying to think of a solution for this problem, the robot took a step out onto the hull, then another.

At first Scott thought Toby was going to tumble all the way to the bottom, and he opened his mouth to protest. The dog was annoying, but he'd grown on him over the years. Toby looked at his open mouth.

"You'll catch flies," Toby said, then began walking down the side of the ship, carefully placing one leg after another.

"I will not," Scott replied, moments before a fly zipped inside his mouth. He gagged and spat it back out. "Gross!"

He'd forgotten the robot's magnetic feet. The same magnets which let him walk around the ship in zero gravity and held him in place during the crash now let him walk slowly and carefully down the side of the Stargazer. Toby reached the ground before Scott did.

The source of the stink was evident immediately. The dragon reeked. Scott wasn't sure how long ago it had died — how long had he been out? But flies and other bugs had already begun working their magic on the neck and head. He didn't want to think about what the rest of the body looked like, buried inside the cone of the ram scoop. Well, mostly buried. As he circled the ship, Scott discovered a claw and a wing that were also exposed.

"What a mess," he said, looking around.

"Ruff," Toby agreed.

The trees were every bit as tall as they'd looked, towering a hundred feet or so above the ground. The tip of the Stargazer's engine stood barely above their tops. Sunlight blasted through the hole his ship had made, but everywhere else the forest floor was gloomy. And wet. It wasn't a swamp, precisely, but Scott could see pools of water scattered about between the trees.

"I think we have company," Toby observed, looking out into the woods.

"Oh, good — rescue at last?" Scott replied, turning around.

A trio of people stood in front of him. They were dressed in clothing that looked like something out of a

Tarzan flick. All three of them held long spears, each with a very sharp looking point.

All three of those points were aimed directly at Scott's chest.

EIGHT

"We come in peace?" Scott said, raising his hands above his head.

This wasn't the welcome he was expecting. No, the humans of the future might not hail him as a heroic figure, but he thought at least he'd be something of a celebrity for a little while. It was like having Magellan show up in the twenty-first century. Or it should have been, anyway.

"Hi?" Scott asked. "Um. Friends? Maybe don't point those things at me? Please?"

His mind raced, trying to figure out what was going on. Some parts of the world had still used spears when he had left Earth, but he'd assumed things would advance enough over the course of a couple hundred years that the practice would have died out. Apparently it was still alive and well, at least where he had the misfortune to land.

These people were Caucasian. They looked to be of European descent, which didn't match up with his memory of any cultures that used spears. Two of the spear-holders were women, one blond and one with red hair. The third was a man whose head was shaved so close you couldn't determine the color. That one pointed past Scott's head, eyes wide.

"Look!" the strange man said.

Well, thank god they spoke English, at least. That would make life a little easier.

"Listen, if you can get me to a phone, or whatever sort of thing you all use to communicate, I can call someone and be on my way. I didn't mean to bother you," Scott said.

The blond woman jabbed at him with her spear, silencing him. The point had barely touched his chest, but it was warning enough. She held her ground, glaring at Scott, and gestured with her head to her companions to go check out whatever the man had seen.

Scott glanced over his shoulder to watch them. They walked over to stand next to the dragon's head. The man jabbed it a couple of times with his spear until the woman with him shoved him, hard. He stumbled, and she laughed, then turned back to face Scott's captor.

"It's a dragon, and it's very dead," the red-haired woman said.

The blond woman with the spear nodded to her and then looked back at Scott. "What happened here?"

"The dragon attacked my ship while I was trying to land. But my ship killed it when I crashed," Scott said. Honesty seemed like the best policy when one had a spear tickling his ribs.

"You killed it?" she asked, in a tone that sounded like she wasn't sure she believed him.

"Well, yes," he replied.

The man pulled a big knife loose from a sheath on his belt and began hacking at the dragon's neck. Scott wasn't sure what he was doing at first, but then the head rolled free from the other ten feet of neck. The man grabbed it by a horn and tried dragging it. The redhead took hold of the other horn. It took both of them to haul the thing even a few feet.

"We'll have to bring back help if we want to haul that to the Keep," the blond woman said. "For now, hack off a horn as proof. We'll bring it along — and him."

Toby chose that moment to step out of the brush, clanking with each step. All three spears shifted direction to aim at him. This was a relief for Scott, who no longer had a pointy thing poking him, but he was worried how the robot might respond to such overt aggression.

He shouldn't have. Toby stopped in place, sat down, dilated his eyes so they were extremely wide, then rolled over on his back, waving his feet in the air and panting.

"Woof!" Toby said.

"It's a dog?" the blond woman asked, glancing back at Scott.

"Yes. My dog. Sorry, I'm sure he didn't mean to startle you," Scott replied.

He wasn't sure how they could take Toby for an ordinary dog. While he was shaped roughly like one, and certainly could sound like one when he wanted to, he didn't have fur. Toby's 'skin' was metal.

"I've never seen a dog like that before," she said.

"He's a one of a kind. Or was, the last time I knew," Scott replied.

She raised her spear and planted the butt into the dirt. "I'm Tamara. We need to get you out of here and back to someplace safe. Our people will want to hear about the dragon and what you did."

"Um, OK, I guess. Do you have a phone there?" he asked her.

She looked at him, her eyes quizzical. "I do not know that word."

"A phone. A communication device. Some way I can get in touch with civilization?" Scott asked.

"Around here, the Keep is civilization. What we have of it. You'll want to come with us. I'll show you what I mean," Tamara said.

"Um," Scott said. He wasn't sure this was a good plan at all.

"You will be safest with us," Tamara said. "Trust me."

He looked into her eyes. Something there said she was a person he could believe in. Scott nodded to her. "All right."

She turned to her companions. "Kendall, Piper, come."

The five of them set off through the forest, massive trees towering overhead. Scott was incredibly impressed by the stature of those towering trunks. He'd never seen anything so large. Redwoods — on the Pacific coast — they were as big as these trees, or close to it. But these weren't coniferous, so he didn't know what they were or where he was.

The first mile was the worst. Scott had been in superb shape before he left, the peak of physical fitness. That was no longer the case after spending two years on a spaceship. The steady acceleration had given him gravity so his muscles hadn't atrophied too badly, but there just wasn't all that much room to run around on the Stargazer. He'd brought a treadmill for just that reason, but he was forced to admit to himself that maybe he hadn't been using it as often as he ought to have been these past six months.

Scott was sweating profusely before they completed the second mile, and the forest was showing no signs of breaking up. There were plenty of life around the place. Bugs as big as his hand buzzed around between the trees, and he spotted a few darting movements slip away between ferns as the party approached.

"How much further are we going?" Scott asked, panting. "And is it always this hot?"

"Another five miles. Not far. It's usually warmer than this, though. It's still spring," Tamara said. "You really aren't from around here, are you?"

"No, I'm not. I've been on a very long trip," Scott said.

How did one explain to a spear-carrying woman that he'd been in space, flying farther from the Earth than any person ever had before? He didn't know what she might know or not know. If he said the wrong thing, she might be offended or think he was lying. Better to play his cards close to his chest until he had a better feel for the place.

Toby froze in place, his head erect. He turned to Scott. "My audio receptors are picking up something strange."

"It spoke!" Kendall said as he aimed his spear at Toby again.

"Yes, he does that sometimes," Scott said. "Toby, what do you hear?"

The robot's audio pickup was far better than his own hearing. If he was picking up something and calling it strange, it was probably worth paying attention to whatever it was.

"Wingbeats."

A moment later a massive roar echoed across the treetops.

NINE

The roar echoed over the treetops. It was coming from somewhere above them. Scott looked up, trying to see through the canopy. Wingbeats sounded overhead.

Was it another dragon? How many of the things were there?

He glanced at his companions, but they'd all crouched down, ducking into the ferns that grew on the forest floor.

Tamara darted up, grabbing Scott by the shoulders and hauling him to the ground. He hit the dirt with a thud and was about to cry out when she slapped a palm over his mouth to silence him.

"Are you crazy? Do you want to get us all killed?" she growled softly in his ear.

Scott could smell the adrenaline in her sweat, the sharp tang that told him she wasn't kidding around. Tamara was scared. He swallowed hard, shaking his head. She removed her hand from his mouth and raised a finger to her lips, gesturing for him to keep quiet.

The wingbeats flew by overhead and faded away back

in the direction of the Stargazer. Scott winced, hoping this other dragon wasn't going to finish the job of eating his ship that the first had begun. There wasn't much he could do about it right now, anyway.

"You must be from far away if you don't know to seek cover when a dragon flies by," Tamara said.

"I'll be honest, I'd never seen a dragon before last night," Scott replied.

"Where you are from, there are no dragons?" Piper asked. "That must be a wonderful place. Is it because you have slain them all? Is that why you came here?"

She seemed very excited about the idea of him killing dragons for them. Getting involved probably wasn't going to be good for his health.

Scott was becoming concerned. One rogue bio-engineered dragon that escaped from a high-tech lab, he could understand. Multiple dragons running around causing enough problems that the humans living here were frightened of them rang all sorts of alarm bells in his head. Something was very wrong.

He was a couple of hundred years in the future, which should have meant that things had gotten better for humanity. Science and technology should be elevated to new levels. But even back in the twenty-first century, Scott was pretty sure flying lizards flapping about on any corner of the planet, no matter how remote, would have warranted a military response.

So where were all the F-22 fighter jets shooting down these big lizards?

Scott glanced at the spear Tamara was holding. The tip was steel, the shaft carefully crafted. But it was just a spear. Even a handgun had to be a better weapon than that. If they were using spears, it was either because they had some bizarre cultural taboo against firearms — or they didn't have any.

What sort of world had he returned to, anyway?

His thoughts kept circling around as they marched, the thinking not really helping Scott reach any conclusions, but it served to keep his mind off his screaming legs. The sooner they were to this Keep, whatever it was, the safer they'd be, apparently. If it was someplace the dragons couldn't chew their way in, he was all for it.

"We're almost there," Piper said, waking him from his brooding.

The woods showed no signs of stopping, but the ground had begun sloping upward and changed from damp to dry dirt. At last they stepped out onto a flatter patch of land, covered in what looked like grey flagstones. A few hundred feet ahead were a pair of arches built into the hillside and bricked over with massive stones, like a set of tunnels someone had sealed off.

"We're here. Welcome to Hero's Keep," Tamara said. She started forward across the flagstones, whistling sharply as she came. Someone half hidden at the top of the stone wall whistled back. Scott gave Toby a glance and then followed Tamara. What other options did he have?

The stones set into the wall were massive, each standing as tall as he was. It must have been hell to move all of them and stack them up like that. They towered all the way to the top of the arches.

At the center base of the wall was a heavy steel door. That was where Tamara was headed, and Scott hurried to catch up.

As they drew closer to the wall, Scott thought the stonework of the arches looked familiar. Two arches tunnels, side by side, rang a bell. Where had he seen that before? He knelt down to examine the flagstone beneath his feet. To his surprise, it wasn't a single stone at all, but a conglomerate. Many smaller rocks were pressed together inside another substrate of darker material.

A flash of color caught his eye. Scott brushed dust off the spot, showing more of the patchy yellow color beneath. Was it some sort of lichen, growing on the stone? He peered more closely.

It wasn't lichen. It was paint.

Scott stood abruptly, staring back the way he'd come. As far as he could see through the thick forest, the flagstones ran in a straight line. Broken chunks of the stuff were everywhere. He turned back to the arches and for the first time knew what he was looking at.

The flagstones were shattered chunks of asphalt. The paint was the last flecks of what had been a center line for a road. And those arches in front of him? Those were the opening of a highway tunnel.

"My god," Scott whispered.

The reason for the lack of communication had become incredibly clear. No one responded to his radio calls because no one still had radio. The Earth he knew was gone. It was replaced by this impossible mess. Dragons flew in the sky and humans ran around wearing loincloths with spears in their hands.

"Are you coming?" Tamara asked. She had already reached the door. Scott nodded dumbly at her, unable to find the words he needed.

All his hopes came crashing down. There was no cure waiting for him here, no high-tech society. He'd dropped onto a planet where the surviving humans weren't even as far along as the Dark Ages.

Scott followed Tamara through the gate, Toby and the

others close behind them. The steel door ground shut after they were through, giving a loud boom as it slid completely into place. The noise had a finality to it, like the tolling of a bell. That was his death knell, Scott figured. He was a dead man walking. Ten years he'd spent, working to fund and create the technology required to build a photon rocket. Two more years in space, soaring across time in the hopes of a cure. All of it for nothing.

The time bomb in his head was still there. He had to be almost out of time. Scott's father was only about ten years older when he started seeing poodles, and the doctors had said it could set in anytime during adulthood, but likely before middle age. Everything he'd gone through to avoid this fate, and now there was no way he could solve the problem.

Scott wanted nothing more than to crawl into a hole and give up. Instead, he followed Tamara into the dark tunnel she called home, wondering what else fate had in store for him today.

TEN

The tunnel was dark and filled with enough smoke that Scott found himself coughing almost immediately. Lamps lit the space, sparsely located along the walls to cast just enough illumination that one wasn't stumbling around completely blind.

That made it difficult to see much, but Scott caught glimpses of a series of small huts to his right. Some of them had small fires out front, with gaunt, frightened-looking people huddled over them.

Tamara ignored it all, pressing onward into the gloom. He wondered where precisely they were headed. Maybe to her place? Or to see whoever was in charge of it all, perhaps. That thought brightened his mood a little. Surely the entire planet couldn't be this bad? Someone would still have working technology, somewhere. Perhaps the leader would be able to direct Scott toward someone who could help him.

"Through here," Tamara said, gesturing ahead. "The smoke is bad, sorry. We can only leave the doors open at night. That vents all the smoke. During the day, the dragons are out."

Scott nodded his understanding. Each torch, campfire, or oil-burning brazier was putting out its own sooty cloud, making the air in the tunnel thick with the stuff.

Tamara led him off to the left, up a series of steps to a closed metal door. A man stood at the door, spear in hand. He made ready to bar their path, but then saw Tamara and relaxed.

"I'm bringing him to my father. He'll want to see this one," she said.

"As you say," the guard replied, stepping clear of her path and holding the door open.

The space inside was a flight of stone steps, leading upward. Tamara took them up the stairs rapidly, Scott and Toby right behind her. The other two people brought up the rear.

"Your father?" Scott asked, huffing a little for breath.

"Yes. He is chief of Heroes Keep," she replied.

Well, that was interesting. At least he'd run into a useful person right off the bat. Her dad was in charge. That made her, what? A princess? Something like that, Scott figured. If she was willing to speak on his behalf, maybe he would be more likely to get help from these people.

The steps stopped at another door. Scott felt a wall. It was rough, cracks running through the stone, but the construction was unmistakable. It was poured concrete, heavily patched over time with other materials. This must have been some sort of access passage in the tunnel, once. How long had the place been used as a residence? He had no way of knowing.

Tamara opened the door and walked out into an open hall with an arched ceiling. The walls here were stone again, but seemed more natural stone and less concrete. Scott had the feeling some of this space had been hewn from rock by hand sometime after the people had taken up residence in the tunnel.

At the far end of the hall was a large table where six men sat, talking with one another. Tamara started forward. As soon as one of them saw her, he stopped speaking and stood. The other men ended their conversation as well but remained seated.

"Father. I've brought someone you should speak with. A stranger to the land," Tamara said.

"I do not have time for foolishness, Tamara. We are discussing war here," the standing man replied.

"Oh, you'll want to speak with this one," she replied with a little more edge to her voice. She was only a few feet from the table now and tossed something through the air.

The dragon horn landed in the middle of the table, clattering loudly as it settled into place.

"What? How?" The standing man took a step back, and Scott thought he lost several shades of color, although it was hard to tell in the dim light.

Tamara pointed at Scott. "He slew a dragon."

That set all the men at the table to whispering with one another. The buzz was loud enough that Scott could easily hear them speaking, but couldn't make out individual words. He looked down at Toby, wondering if the dog was able to pick up more.

"Woof," Toby replied, nodding.

Sometimes, the robot was better at predicting what Scott needed than he expected. He flashed a smile at the dog. Toby would fill him in on any word he'd picked up later. Well, that was assuming he'd actually understood the semi-silent language. It could also be that Toby was agreeing with something entirely different. One never knew with robots.

"Is this true?" The standing man, who must be their chief, stepped around the others and came forward. He eyed Scott up and down. "He doesn't look like much of a warrior."

That got under Scott's skin more than he thought it would. Not much of a warrior? He had taken self-defense classes, fenced in college, and spearfished with great white sharks. Although the latter was by accident, but that was another story entirely. He had plenty of martial experience and wanted to say so.

Toby caught his eye. The dog shook its head almost imperceptibly.

It wanted him to keep quiet. Well, Scott didn't think so.

"I killed it," Scott said.

Toby let out a sigh.

"So, you are a dragonslayer," the chief said, walking a circle around Scott. "Where is your spear? Your shield?"

"Father, the bright light we saw last night was his spear. It was a massive spear, hurled from the sky to stab into the ground. With that, he slew the dragon — smashed it to the ground and cut off its head."

Well, that was most of the truth. Of course, killing the thing had been an accident, but Scott figured these people didn't need to know that. They seemed very interested in him as a dragonslayer. If they knew he'd done it by accident, he might lose whatever limited celebrity status that had won for him.

"Yes, but I am new here. I was seeking a place that had a treasure I need very badly," Scott said. "Do you know how to get to California? Or at least where it might be from here? I'm afraid I don't know at all."

The chief snapped a look at the wall. Something hung there. "Bring the map, Poltius."

One of the other men stood from the table and carefully removed the map from the wall. As he brought it closer, Scott realized that it was a map of the old United States, laminated with plastic. It was yellowed with age, torn and carefully mended, but it still showed everything.

Or almost everything, anyway. Someone had taken blue paint and blurred out the edge of the New England coastline.

Poltius laid the map out on the table. Scott stepped up to the thing and tapped on the spot that was California. "That's it. That's where I need to go. Where are we?"

The chief strode forward and tapped Connecticut, near where the blue paint had been added. "This is our Keep, here."

Scott let out a frustrated sound. There were over three thousand miles of continent between him and where he had to go.

ELEVEN

Of all the awful luck, Scott figured his had to be the worst. He looked down at the map, running his fingers over the massive distance between the two points. The map was telling him as clear as day what sort of journey he had ahead. On foot? It was impossible. With his ship, perhaps he could get to Berkeley. That was probably his only hope.

That was assuming he could still find the cure when he got out there. After all, if things were this bad here, who knew what they were like elsewhere? It was a long shot, but it seemed the only option he had left.

He glanced around at the people gathered at the table. They were dirty and tired-looking, but despite that, they had a vitality about them he'd only seen among surfers and other athletes back home. These were people used to hard work. And to fighting as well, judging by how the guards held their weapons.

"Are things like this everywhere?" Scott asked, hoping to hear some good news for a change. Maybe civilization had continued unabated elsewhere?

"Oh, no. Not at all," the chief replied.

"Thank goodness…" Scott started to say. If he could get in touch with another place with higher tech, repairing the ship should be a breeze.

"Most of the other tribes nearby are in much worse shape than we are," the chief went on. "We're much stronger than the rest."

Scott sighed. Of course this was the best around. It still might not be the best anywhere, but if they hadn't even heard rumors of a group with tech, then there might just be none left. That left him up a creek without a paddle.

"Toby, you think we can get the ship repaired and airborne without help?" Scott asked, tapping the map in thought.

"Woof," Toby replied. He whipped his tail against the floor excitedly.

Scott looked over at him sharply. He'd been expecting something more than that from the robot. But maybe it was best if the dog not act like a person too much. He recalled Kendall's reaction. Some of these people might act before they thought if they became alarmed. Toby would be tough to break, but he wasn't invulnerable.

"That is the strangest dog I have ever seen," the chief said. "May I touch him?"

Scott glanced at Toby, who rolled his eyes and gave a tiny nod. He was playing the role of a dog for now, but that wouldn't last.

"Sure," Scott said.

The chief ran his fingers over the dog's head and back. He peered down intently at the robot, then flipped his hand over and rapped with his fingers. Toby jumped at the movement and came to step behind Scott.

"Sorry. I was just curious. He has a metal shell, like steel but shinier. It is an armor of some sort?" the chief asked.

"No, chief. It's the skin of this sort of dog. Toby is from my home, and special to me," Scott said.

"Hector," the chief replied. When Scott looked confused, he added "My name is Hector. I'm the chief here, but nobody calls me that. So, you plan to repair your — ship, you said? A boat of some sort?"

Scott wasn't sure how much he ought to reveal. If he told these people everything, would they even believe him? On the other hand, they'd already seen his ship fall from the sky, so they'd be inclined to believe at least part of the truth. It didn't make sense to keep secrets they already knew, and maybe he could win some trust by offering information.

"A ship that flies," Scott said. "Or did, before the dragon ate part of it."

"Ah, the dragon you slew?" Hector asked.

"Yes."

"And how exactly did you manage it?" Hector said. His eyes narrowed and a little menace trickled into his voice. "I'm only asking because you should know that in living memory, no one has ever slain a dragon."

"Father, the dragon was dead, buried under his ship," Tamara said. "I saw it with my own eyes."

"So you said," Hector replied. "But no one has told me how it was done. You'll understand my skepticism."

"I used a device on my ship to kill it," Scott said. That was mostly true. Without the ram scoop catching the dragon's tail, Scott figured it would have flown away rather than being impaled by the ship. "But it's probably broken along with the rest of the vessel. It's going to take a lot of work to get her flying again."

Hector ran his fingers through his beard, nodding. "I

think I understand the situation, then. You came from some-place far off, in this flying ship. You used a weapon on the ship to kill the dragon, which in turn damaged your ship before it died."

"That pretty much sums it up," Scott said. He glanced at Tamara, wondering why there was such a worried look on her face. The frown, too, what was that about?

"A weapon like that would be incredibly useful to have around," Hector said.

"I can see why you'd say that, sure," Scott agreed. He was starting to have a bad feeling about how this conversa-tion was turning. "But like I said, it's trashed."

"And like you said, perhaps it can be repaired," Hector said.

"Did I say that?" Scott chuckled nervously. The last time he'd felt like this, he was being held up at the ATM in downtown Cincinnati at midnight. This little interview had the same vibe.

He backed up a step. Two guards were between him and the door.

"You did," Hector said. He nodded. "You should be aware, my people live close to the ocean."

Something struck Scott in the back of the head. Dizzy and unable to keep himself up, he tumbled forward onto the floor. As the darkness overtook him, the last thing he heard was Hector saying, "We are very good at fixing boats."

TWELVE

Scott stared at the picture on his phone, looking to the image for strength and courage. It was almost done — his rocket. He couldn't believe the thing was finally nearing completion. It had taken five years. But by god, it was at long last almost done. There was one last thing he had to deal with. Of all his worries over the course of the project, this had been the biggest. It was the one hurdle he'd dreaded more than any other.

The house in front of him was elegant. Rose bushes lined the walk on either side. Scott knew from experience that their thorns were as sharp as their flowers were beautiful. This was entirely appropriate, since their owner had similar qualities.

He mustered his courage and climbed the steps up to the old oak door, but his finger wavered over the doorbell button. Did he have the strength to manage this? Scott swallowed hard. He'd been so certain before, but now that he was actually facing the danger, he wasn't so sure.

In fact, this could definitely be done another day. No need to take care of this particular matter now. He could definitely come back another time. Scott turned to go, planning to beat a hasty retreat back to his motorcycle, when the door opened.

"Scott! So good to see you," the woman in the doorway said.

"Hi, Mom. Good to see you, too," Scott replied.

He tried to cover up that he'd been about to flee, but he was pretty sure she'd noticed. She turned away, flowing back into the house. Scott winced. This wasn't starting well.

"Come, sit," his mother said, taking a seat on the large sofa in the front room and patting the cushion next to her.

"You're looking well, Mom," Scott said as he checked around for someplace to sit that put him outside arm's reach. There was an easy chair just across from where she sat that ought to do nicely. He plopped himself down.

She frowned at him. Olivia Free wasn't used to being thwarted. Getting her way in life was second nature to her and always had been. Scott wasn't like that; everyone told him he was more like his Dad. Bjorn had been a carefree adventurer, wandering the world in search of his next epic stunt.

Where Bjorn had been flighty, Liv had been stolid. Where he had been buoyant, she had been stern. Scott had to admit that it was his mother who had the lion's share of the brains in the family, however. He often wished that he'd inherited more of that brilliance from her, but he had long since despaired at ever coming even close.

"You've got a trip planned, I hear," his mother said. That snapped Scott's mind right back to the subject at hand. How had she heard? More importantly, precisely what had she heard?

"Yes, Mom. I have. I wanted to come see you before I

left," Scott said. "I'm going to be gone quite a while, you see."

She blinked her eyes at him. Scott half-smiled. His mother wasn't very good at pretending to be vapid. She knew it, too, which meant she was toying with him. That was OK. Mom in a playful mood was better than Mom in an angry one.

"You know everything, don't you?" Scott said.

His mother snapped a single nod.

"You've been following every step of my project's progress since I first started, haven't you?" Scott asked. Again, he already knew the answer.

She nodded a second time. "I was only wondering when — or even if — you planned to tell me. I'm glad you did, Scott."

She smiled, and it was a real smile that lit up her face this time, not a plastic put-on one. This smile went all the way to her eyes, which were shining with unshed tears.

"I'm proud of you," she said.

Scott's jaw dropped. Of all the responses he'd expected from his mother, this was last on the list. He'd anticipated anger, at having burned so much of the family fortune on this adventure. Or fury because he was leaving her behind, not for a little while, but forever. Once Scott left, he would never see his mother again.

To the best of his knowledge, his mother had never said those words before.

"Oh, shut your mouth before you catch flies," she snapped, sounding much more like the mother he knew well. "Yes, I'm proud of you. Damn it, son! It isn't every mother whose child invents the fastest spaceship ever built."

"I didn't so much invent it—"

"—As invest in its invention. I know all about it, remember?" she replied. "Still, you had the vision to understand what the photon rocket could do, and the drive to accomplish your goal. That's a side of you that you've never shown me before."

"Your father's influence, I suspect," she went on. "Oh, I loved Bjorn. His zest for life made mine better every day he was in it. But if the man had one most infuriating trait about him, it was his inability to strive for... well, anything. Most things came easily to him. To you as well. Those things that came hard, he simply avoided."

Scott had done much the same thing. He'd briefly won enthusiastic support from his mother after being accepted to Harvard at eighteen. But when he dropped out six months later, she had been much less pleased with him. Those courses had been hard! Besides, what did he need a college degree for, if he was just going to follow in his father's footsteps and travel about on adventures? Skydiving, deep sea exploring, polar treks — the world was his oyster.

Until it wasn't anymore. Watching his father lose his mind had been the hardest thing Scott had ever endured. Was his mother right? Had something changed inside him? He didn't feel any different, but his Mom was a perceptive woman.

"The ship is ready to go. I'll be leaving soon. It's a two-year trip," Scott said.

"For you, perhaps. How long for us you leave behind?" she asked.

"Two hundred years."

The silence hung between them in the room like a shroud. An apt analogy; once he left, he would effectively be dead to her, and she to him. While they'd both live on, it would be in completely separate lives.

"I've made you something," his mother said, sniffling a little. She clapped her hands twice.

"Oh, Mom, you didn't have to. Really!" Scott said. He was imagining what it could be. His mother's craft projects were things of legend. Once, he'd worn one into school as a child. The other children in class had sworn the thing was giving them headaches. The girl right behind him ran from the class to vomit in the bathroom. Mr. Humbert politely asked him to remove the sweater and pack it away before exiting the room just as swiftly as the girl had.

That was the end of wearing Mom's presents anywhere. After that day, Scott had carefully said thank-you for each one, and then just as carefully packed them away someplace where they would never be seen by the eyes of mortal men again.

Some things were too terrible to leave loose in the world.

"It's not what you're thinking," his mother snapped. If she knew about the project, then damn it, she probably knew about the Secret Sweater Depot, as well. How many more of his secrets had she guessed? It didn't pay to have a genius for a mother.

"Woof."

Scott jumped halfway out of his seat. A metal dog was sitting on the floor beside him.

"Um, good boy?" he said, hesitant.

"Thank you. I like to think I am a better boy than you. Imagine, turning to walk away from your own mother's door," the dog said.

Scott's eyes were as wide as saucers as he turned back to face his mother. "It talks."

"Yes, indeed he does," she replied, stressing the pronoun. "Toby here is useful in all sorts of ways. I had him built specially for your trip once I knew the full scope of what you were doing. You'll need someone out there to keep you company in space for two years. And you never know just what you'll come back to when you return. Having an ally you can trust will be a boon, I'm sure."

"Thanks, mom," Scott said. This time, it was heartfelt. Of all the gifts she'd given him, Toby had to be the coolest.

THIRTEEN

Tamara felt for a pulse in the stranger's neck and found one. She hadn't been sure, at first. She glared up at Kraig, the small club still in his meaty hands.

"He's alive. Did you have to hit him so hard?" Tamara asked.

Kraig just shrugged and turned away. He wasn't known for his thinking ability, but he was a big man and hit hard. All good reasons for her father to keep him on his personal enforcer squad. She got back to her feet and turned to her father and chief.

"That wasn't necessary. He was already cooperating with us," Tamara said.

"Yes, but he isn't from our Keep. How can we trust him to have our interests at heart?" Hector said. "Look at his clothing and at his dog. Does it make you wonder what other amazing things might be waiting back on his ship? It should. This could be the thing that saves our people."

"It's wrong, father. To strike a person who came to us as a guest is wrong. To steal from him is wrong."

Hector waved aside her concerns. "There is no wrong when it is for the good of our Keep and our people."

Tamara disagreed, but didn't know how to convince her father. There were some lines you simply didn't want to ever cross, no matter how dire the situation. It felt like they were crossing them all the time now, though. Survival at any cost was the new normal. But were they really surviving if they sacrificed everything that mattered about themselves in the process?

"Take him to the lower holding cells," Hector said.

Two of his guards picked Scott up under his arms and dragged him from the room. Those cells were tiny, dark, and wet. He would wake up alone and knowing only that he'd been betrayed. Tamara hated every bit of it.

"I told him he would be safe with us," she said.

"You should not have done so," Hector replied.

"But this smears my honor now."

"Not so. He will be safe. In a cell. While we figure out what to do with him."

Tamara turned away and stared at a wall.

"My daughter, you are angry. Don't be. Someday, all of these decisions will rest on your shoulders instead of mine. Then you'll better see why sometimes the hard decisions are necessary for the good of our people," Hector said.

"If you say so, father," Tamara replied.

She didn't think she could ever be so cold about harming someone else. Tamara would fight when it was needful, but that was always against an active threat. The idea of striking an unarmed man down from behind when he was visiting under a promise of security disgusted her. She didn't think time or duty would change her feelings on the subject.

"We will leave at first light to investigate this stranger's boat," Hector said, speaking now to the others assembled in the room. He ignored Tamara as he spoke.

"It's not a boat," Tamara said. "More like a tower. It resembles the towers in the ancient cities."

"But he said it was a boat?" Hector replied, his brows knitting together.

"A ship. He said it was a ship that flew. A tower that came from the heavens," Tamara said.

"All the more reason to explore it and plumb its secrets. We will bring the dog along as well," Hector said. "As insurance, but also in case it might be useful."

He rapped his knuckles on Toby's head. They rang like a soft bell on the metal plating.

"Remarkable creature. You will behave, won't you boy?" Hector asked the dog.

"Woof," Toby said, wagging his tail.

Hector laughed. "I thought so. Good. I will need some of my guardsmen. Kraig, see to assembling a team."

The big man nodded and left the room.

"I'd like to come along as well, father," Tamara said.

"I think that might not be wise," Hector said.

"But I found the ship. I've spoken to your prisoner. If anyone should be able to find the secrets of his ship, it would be me," Tamara protested.

"You are too close to this, daughter. It might be dangerous, as well. I can't risk both of us on the same venture," Hector said. "No, you will remain here, taking my place as leader until I return."

"But..."

"That is my final word. You are dismissed," Hector said.

When he spoke like that, more protest would only cause him to dig his heels in deeper. Talking about it further wasn't going to make things any better. Tamara closed her mouth, making her face a mask to hide her anger.

"May I go then, father?" she asked.

"You may."

She turned and left the room. It was maddening, a smear on her personal honor that he'd done as he had. The stranger had expected to be their guest, a hero for having killed a dragon. Instead, he'd been assaulted and imprisoned.

But what could she do about it? There were few options open to her. Tamara returned to her quarters and tried to rest, but sleep came very slowly and wasn't restful when it did. Her dreams were full of dragons chasing her down for having betrayed the man from the sky.

She woke still exhausted after what felt like only a few hours. Tamara dressed and stepped from her room back into the great tunnel. Like her father, her quarters were in the warren of passages which ran between the twin tunnels where most of her people dwelled.

Scant daylight poured in through cracks in the defensive wall. The tunnel spent most of each daylight period in a barely-lit gloom. She preferred to be above ground, living in the light. It would help clear her thoughts at least.

Tamara made her way to the watch-tower where a guard stood at his duty post, watching for danger to the Keep. He nodded to her but didn't interfere with her passage past his post. There were some benefits to being the chief's daughter. One of them was having relatively free run of the entire Keep.

Movement out near the forest caught her eye. A large patrol was just leaving her line of sight, vanishing between the mighty trunks. That had to be her father. They were off to the ship already. They'd arrive soon, and wreak who-knew-what sort of havoc on the place.

It was a bitter thought, that her word to the stranger had been broken. But what could she do? Her father still ruled. Could she go against his wishes?

Tamara stood there watching until the last person vanished from sight, all the while thinking hard. Only drastic action might redeem her honor now, but if she acted against her father in this, he might never forgive her.

"Which is greater to me, my honor or my security?" Tamara whispered into the wind.

It didn't take her long to come up with the answer to that question. Regardless of what else came of it, her honor demanded action. Even if that action cost her everything, she could not stand idly by and watch this wrongdoing without taking a stand against it.

She loved her father, but he was wrong. This decision was wrong. She would find a way to show him that, to open his eyes to the truth. Or perhaps she would fail. But either way, her honor would be intact.

Decided on her course, Tamara stepped from the wall back into the gloom of the tunnel. She had a mission to perform, and a promise to fulfill.

FOURTEEN

The pounding headache wasn't new. If anything, Scott was becoming used to gradually waking back up to a splitting skull. It was happening far too often these days.

"Ugh," he mumbled. It was about as coherent as he could manage.

The surroundings were new, however. He lay on a cold stone floor. The rock was rough-hewn under his fingers. He tried to get to his feet and couldn't. They were bound together with rough rope, as were his hands.

Only a little light illuminated the cell where they'd tossed him, shining from somewhere outside through slits in the door. Scott looked around the small space. There wasn't much to see. The room was barely long enough for him to lie down lengthwise and was half as wide. It wasn't high enough to stand up in even if he wasn't tied up.

"I've been tossed in a closet," Scott said.

Toby was nowhere to be seen. Scott felt a rush of real anger at that. Hector must have his dog. Toby was his damned dog, a present from his mother. And that asshole had taken Toby away and locked him in a closet.

"We'll just have to see about that," Scott grumbled.

The first step had to be freeing his hands and feet. Fortunately, that part shouldn't be too hard.

The walls were even rougher stone than the floor. Scott scooched his way to the back wall and felt around, looking for a sharp spot. It took a bit of fumbling in the dark, but he managed. Then it was just a matter of slowly rubbing the ropes against the rock until they frayed.

Hands free, Scott shook them out to get full feeling back in the digits. Those ropes had been far tighter than they needed to be! Then he untied the knots binding his feet. He coiled that rope and slipped it into a pocket. It might be useful later.

That was one plus. They'd left him in his suit from the ship. He hadn't brought much along with him. There hadn't really been time, what with the spear-carrying people accosting him. But he still had a few tricks up his sleeve. One of them was the radio in his collar. He keyed the microphone.

"Toby, can you hear me?" Scott asked.

No response. He felt a moment of fear for Toby's safety, but he didn't think these people would have done anything to harm the robot. He was obviously valuable. They weren't going to risk breaking him. No, it was more likely that he was just deep enough underground that the transmissions weren't reaching his dog.

Time to try the door. Scott went over and carefully shoved on the thing, but it was barred or locked on the other side. He'd figured it would be, but it was worth checking. How best to unlock a cell door? He felt like he was in one of those survivor TV shows, where the contestants had to come up with cunning solutions to problems laid before them.

Except a lot more was riding on this game than a paycheck. Toby's safety, his life, his future — everything counted on the decisions he made in the next little while.

The thought should have scared the shit out of him, but Scott found the idea oddly liberating instead. His mother had been right after all. Not really a shock, that. She usually was.

All his life, Scott had been doing things that were easy for him. Quick success, little chance of failure, and no cost involved even if he did fail. The rocket trip had been something else. If it had failed, he would have died. One way or another, whether it exploded or just didn't work, he would've been dead from the blast or his disease. That sense of purpose and real danger had tasted sweet.

He'd lost that sense over most of the last two years. The ship was boring 99.9 percent of the time, and about to kill him the other fraction of a percent. Long periods of boredom punctuated by brief moments of absolute terror. Where had he heard that before?

But now that he was back on Earth, he felt alive again all the time. These problems mattered, from the dragon to being imprisoned in this cell. Failure was going to have nasty consequences. It felt good to have his decisions matter.

Scott wondered if that made him a little crazy.

He took stock of what he had. The suit and its radio. The rope he'd collected from his legs, and the fragments of rope that had bound his hands. The suit itself was sort of a tool, too. It was laced with tubes to help support his body temperature in both hot and cold environments. It also had a small tool packet inserted into a slot on his arm.

The tools weren't much. Just a set of small, flat, metal devices designed to handle basic maintenance in an emergency. Scott could see the size of the bar holding his cell shut when he peeked through the crack. It had to weigh at least twenty or thirty pounds. There was no way he was moving that with a sliver of metal like the screwdriver from his kit.

"Give me a big enough lever, and I can move the world," Scott mused.

The screwdriver might not move the bar by itself, but as part of a system? He had a tiny wire cutter in the kit as well. Using that, he sliced up the bits of torn rope into smaller chunks. Then he slid the wire cutters into the crack at the top of the door, packing them carefully into place with the shredded rope.

Once that was fairly secure, he took the other rope from his pocket and tied a loop in one end. Then he tried pushing the loop through the crack at the edge of the door. It was close. The knot didn't want to pass, at first. He had to take it back out and carefully retie the loop to make the knot as small as possible.

This time it slipped out and dangled down over the bar. Scott paused a moment, hoping there wasn't anyone standing outside watching him do all this work. If there was, he'd probably know about it soon enough. He gave it about thirty seconds. Nobody started laughing at him, so he figured he was safe to proceed. He looped the other end of his rope up over the wire-cutters.

Scott slid the screwdriver underneath the bar. Then he hooked the loop over the far side of the screwdriver. He pulled on the rope until he had tension, the rope running from the looped screwdriver up to the wire-cutters and then back down to his hand.

"A lever alone won't work. But a lever and a pulley?" Scott said. "By Jove, I think we've got it!"

He pulled on the rope, adding tension. The far end of the screwdriver went up. He lifted the near end as well, keeping it even with the end lifted by the rope. The first few inches weren't hard, but by the time it was six inches up, Scott was sweating. How high was he going to need to lift this thing?

At a foot, Scott was nearing the end of his strength. Pulling the rope wasn't hard, but holding up the inside edge of the screwdriver was painful. The tool was biting into his hand, and every second felt like it was going to slice him open. He gave one more massive effort, jerking the rope down and pushing up with his palm at the same time. The bar lifted another six inches and then tumbled away.

The door slipped open a couple of inches, but the bar smashed into the floor with a crash that had to have carried outside.

FIFTEEN

There wasn't much time. Someone would've heard that noise. Scott shoved hard on the door. It moved only a few more inches. The bar was on the floor, making a scraping sound as it slid over each bump in the rock floor. Scott sighed. There was no way to keep this quiet. He pushed again, even harder.

The door ground open. As it did, the wire-cutters fell and almost hit him in the head. Scott quickly stashed them, the rope, and his other tools back into a pocket while checking out the room.

Except it wasn't a room. It was a short hallway with two more doors set into the same wall as the one he'd just escaped from. More cells? What if Toby was trapped in one? The only available light was from an oil lamp halfway down the passage. It was just enough that he might be able to peer into the other cells without opening them.

He raced to the next cell door and peered through the gap on the side. Nobody was immediately visible.

"Toby?" he whispered. No answer. The third door was the same. Apparently he was the only prisoner down there.

The passage ended in another door. Scott cast about for anything that looked like a weapon. There really wasn't much he could use on the cell block. The oil lamp might start a small fire, but it was a crappy weapon. The bar which had held his cell closed? He tried picking it up.

The thing was as heavy as it looked. Solid iron, and it had to be at least twenty pounds. He wasn't sure he could swing it more than a few times, but it was better than nothing.

Scott went to the door and placed a hand on the ring set into its wooden face. The best tool he had was the element of surprise. No one would expect him to escape so quickly and so soon, he figured. One hand gripping the bar as tight as he could, he swung the door open as fast as he could.

Tamara was standing there, her hand raised as if she was about to open the door herself. Her glance went to his face, then down his arm to the metal bar. Without missing a beat, Tamara lashed out with her right foot, striking Scott's left wrist — the arm that was holding the bar. His fingers went numb, and he couldn't maintain his grip anymore. The bar clattered to the floor again.

"Ow!" he said, gripping his wounded arm.

"What are you doing?" Tamara asked.

"What's it look like? I'm escaping! Why are you here?" Scott asked her.

She chuckled. "To help you escape. But it appears I was almost too late to do so. Come. Follow me."

Tamara turned away and walked down the passage, her footfalls rapid and silent. Scott wasn't sure what to make of it. Was she telling him the truth? Or just leading him to more guards so they could take him prisoner again?

If it was the latter, she could just do the job herself.

That kick hurt! She wouldn't have a hard time taking him down, and she probably knew it. That meant she most likely was really trying to help. The question was then why — but that could be answered once he was out of this place.

Scott followed along in her trail. He was nowhere near as quiet as Tamara, and kept scuffing his feet on random rough patches of the floor. Every time he did, she looked back at him and held a finger to her lips. Yes, he knew they needed to be quiet. He was trying!

"Here," Tamara said, kneeling down. "Put this on. It will hide some of your strangeness."

She held up a shoulder to floor woven garment that looked more like an oversized dress than anything else. Scott held it up and eyed it. Then he looked over at Tamara.

"Is this a dress? Because it looks like a dress," he said.

"Put it on!" she hissed, her eyes flashing.

Scott grumbled but did as she bid. The cloth was smelly, but it did have a hood that helped keep his face hidden. In the relative darkness of the main tunnel, he would barely be noticed. That was the easy part, though. What about the guards at the door?

The main tunnel was as dark as he recalled. Two sets of armed men marched past them, hurrying on their way to some post or job. Neither of the pairs seemed to take much notice of Scott, although one man did call out to them as they passed.

"Good day, ladies," he said.

Scott waited until they were well gone before whispering to Tamara. "This is a dress, isn't it!"

"Yes. Once they know you're gone, they'll be looking for a man, not a woman. No one who just passed you will recall you," Tamara said. "It's the best disguise."

She wasn't wrong. Scott had to admit it was a pretty smart idea, to be honest. Nobody was paying them any attention at all as they marched through the tunnel, passing patches of little dwellings on either side of the main path.

That was about to change, though. Up ahead was the gate. Scott didn't see how the dress could possibly hide him from the eyes of the guard there.

But when they arrived, there was no guard. Scott looked about, but didn't see him anywhere. "How?"

"Piper owed me a favor," Tamara said. "She's lured Petyr away and is no doubt currently making him a very happy man. Although once my father finds out he was gone from his post, he'll wish he'd been more dutiful."

"Why? You've gone to all this effort to get me loose. You're bound to get in trouble, too. Why help me?" Scott asked.

"Because it was wrong of my father to do as he did. Our desperation does not excuse such treatment of a guest to our home," Tamara said. "I am acting only as I think he would act, if he were not so afraid."

Afraid of what? Nothing she was saying made much sense. Was her father scared of dragons? If that was the case, wouldn't getting the brand new dragon slayer on his side be better than beating him up and locking him in a cell? Scott was missing part of this story.

But before he could ask any more questions, she opened the gate and led the way out. At the exit, Tamara placed a hand on Scott's chest, glancing both ways before allowing him out.

"No guards. Come on!" she said. She pulled him out of the exist passage, then shut the door again. It closed with a clang as the locking mechanism swung back into place. Then she dashed off toward the forest.

Scott took off after her. He was free! It had been even easier than he'd thought it would be. But freedom was only the beginning. Toby was still in there somewhere. He had to get his dog back. Then he had to see about getting his ship ready to leave this god-forsaken armpit.

SIXTEEN

They'd been running for long enough that Scott had lost his way in the woods. The towering trees blocked his line of sight, so he couldn't even see landmarks to navigate from. He had no idea how Tamara was finding her way around, but without her he'd be lost.

Finally, tired and worried, he stopped and called out to her. "Wait."

"What?" she replied, all but tapping her foot on the ground. "I need to get you to safety and then get back before I am missed."

"Where are you taking me? Where is Toby? Why are you helping me in the first place?" Scott asked all three questions rapid-fire.

"I told you, I am helping you because my father is wrong. As for the rest? I am hoping to get you back to your ship before my father gets there with his repair crew. They left at first light, but they are carrying tools, equipment, and supplies, so they're moving slowly."

Oh, that wasn't good. Scott didn't know what they would make of a rocket ship, but he was fairly secure in the idea that they had no prayer of fixing it. Any repairs they made would only make his job more difficult. Still, there might be a way to get them to back off...

"What about Toby?" he asked.

"The dog? My father has him. He seemed too valuable to leave behind," Tamara said. "Now enough of this. We still have another mile to go. Come on!"

She turned and rushed off again, her pace a steady but light jog. Tamara looked like she could keep that up for hours. Scott was again wishing he'd spent more hours on the treadmill. He was huffing a little, but at least he was keeping up with her.

Then she was slowing down. Scott stopped when Tamara raised her hand. She crept forward, one foot at a time, and peered out from behind a tree. She looked down the hill from their position for what felt like a long time. Then she turned back to Scott, holding one finger to her lips while beckoning him closer with the other hand.

Scott went to join her, making as little noise as he could through the underbrush. It wasn't easy, and he winced every time a twig snapped. At last he was leaning against the trunk beside Tamara.

"They beat us here," Tamara said.

Was that a hint of accusation in her voice? Scott sighed and looked around the edge of the tree. Sure enough, Hector and a dozen of his goons were down there. They were unrolling leather wraps filled with metal tools. Damn, it looked like they really did have the stuff on hand to at least do some damage to his ship. Enough blows from one of those hammers in the right places, and the Stargazer would be nothing but scrap.

"I've got to stop them," Scott said. "They'll destroy my ship. It's my only shot at getting where I need to go."

Tamara shrugged. "How? Two against a dozen isn't a good fight."

"We have Toby, too," Scott said.

"I was counting him. You think I'm joining you in getting a beating from my father? Ha! I don't think so," Tamara replied.

Scott chuckled and rubbed his sore head where one of the guards had clubbed him earlier. "I guess I can't blame you for that. You did a lot just by helping me get out. Good luck, then."

"Wait — that's it? You're going in by yourself anyway? You're going to get yourself killed one of these days, Scott Free."

"Probably. But in the meantime, I have a best friend to rescue. No matter what else, I'm not leaving Toby behind."

He did have an idea. The radio was really close to his dog now. It would almost certainly work. Scott keyed the microphone.

"Hey old dog. Wanna learn some new tricks?" Scott asked.

"Scott? Oh, thank god. If I have to pretend to be as dumb as an ordinary dog for even one more minute, my circuits are going to overload. Do you have any idea—"

Scott cut him off. "We'll get you loose, don't worry. They still think you're a normal dog?"

"As normal as a dog made of metal can be, I suppose. I'm broadcasting to you only, no local audio. I've been playing dumb so far," Toby said. "But if they keep offering me bones, I'm going to bite one of them."

Scott stifled a laugh. It wouldn't do to give away his position. It might come down to a fight, at that. If he couldn't scare these people away, he'd have to choose between losing the ship and fighting them. Luckily, they didn't seem to know much at all about technology. He was pretty sure he could scare them.

"Toby, you have a good uplink to the ship?" Scott asked over their radio.

"What is an uplink? How are you speaking to Toby?" Tamara whispered beside him.

Whoops, he'd forgotten she was there. "I'll explain as soon as I can."

Toby responded. "Yes, I'm ten feet away. I have a strong connection to the central computer."

"Good. Remember that music I was playing when we were fighting the dragon?" Scott asked.

"Yes, I recall the dreadful din coming from the speakers as we plummeted to our almost-certain deaths," Toby replied. "It's indelibly etched on my RAM."

"I don't think you can indelibly etch RAM—" Scott started to say.

"Metaphor, my dear boy," Toby said. "Anyway, you want to play that now?"

It ought to work. The ship had external speakers, and they were capable of putting out some decent volume. "Yeah, I want you to play it on the ship's outside speakers. And Toby? I want you to crank it."

"Ah. I think I see the plan," the robot replied. "Executing in ten seconds."

Scott turned back to Tamara. "You're going to want to cover your ears."

"Why?"

"Just trust me! Do it quick," Scott said. Then he followed his own advice and clapped his hands over his ears to protect them from what was coming. He saw Tamara do the same just in time.

The sound rolled over the valley and up the hillsides

like a solid wall. It was enough volume to shake smaller tree branches, vibrate the low-growing brush, and knock thousands of leaves down from the trees in a sudden rain.

It was also enough volume to pretty much instantly disable any human being caught in the vicinity. The few nearest to the ship collapsed on the ground, hands over their ears. The ones farther away had time to cover their ears and flee, but Scott figured even they would have lost their hearing for the next little while. Even with his hands pressed firmly over his ears, the noise was uncomfortably loud.

All at once, it stopped. Scott stood up and uncovered his ears. Toby barked from near the ship. He looked back at Tamara.

"Are you OK?" Scott asked.

She nodded a reply, still looking dazed. Scott saw a drop of blood drip from her ear and swore. She must have been just a little slow in covering them and gotten part of the blast. That would be a busted eardrum or worse. He could treat it on the ship, but that would mean bringing Tamara on board. That was an added complexity he hadn't counted on.

Still, she could go deaf if he didn't get the injury treated soon, and it would be his fault. After she'd helped him, he didn't feel right about leaving her to her fate.

"Come on!" Scott said. Then he grabbed her hand, and the two of them rushed down the hill toward the waiting ship.

SEVENTEEN

"Toby, get the ship opened up!" Scott shouted as he ran down the hill.

He saw the robot's jaw moving, so he was clearly responding with something, but it wasn't reaching Scott's ears. Even with his hands helping, the sound had still messed up his hearing!

Three of Hector's men lay on the ground. One of them was unconscious. The other two were holding their ears and wearing pained expressions on their faces. They weren't going to come after him too soon, but it was just a matter of time before they got over the stun and were back on their feet. Scott needed to be back in the ship by then.

He reached Toby, Tamara still in tow. The dog said something again. This time Scott could hear that Toby was speaking words, but couldn't quite make out what they were through the ringing in his ears.

"I can't hear you," Scott said.

"How about now?" Toby replied. He was clearly audible again!

"Much better! What did you do?"

"I've increased the decibels of my speakers into a range you can hear. We shouldn't do this for long; it will slow your ears' recovery," Toby replied.

"Got it. Ship open?" Scott asked.

Toby nodded. Then he looked at Tamara. "Is she coming with us?"

"Yup. The blast hurt her. Have to use the med-bay to fix her up."

"Are you really sure that's a good idea? Her father ordered you bludgeoned not too many hours ago," Toby asked.

He had a point. It was Tamara who'd led him to her father in the first place. Her fault he'd been hit and imprisoned. But it was also she who had helped him escape. Scott figured he owed her.

"She helped me get out of there and back to you," Scott said.

"If you're sure," Toby said. Scott swore he saw the robot roll its eyes. Then Toby started up the side of the ship, one magnetic foot after another.

Scott looked back at Tamara. Her eyes were wide, mouth open, gaping up at the robot as he ascended. Scott wanted to laugh. It was such a common sight for him, but the idea of a dog walking twenty feet up a sheer metal wall must be amazing to these people.

"We have to go up the hard way, unfortunately," Scott said. He knew she couldn't hear him, but he motioned to the ladder rungs and mimed climbing up. She nodded and grabbed hold, then began climbing. Scott started up after her and tried not to be distracted by the view he was getting.

Tamara seemed to think of this partway up and glared down at him. Scott put on his most innocent expression and waved her upward. They had to hurry. The guys on the ground were already getting back up. The ones who'd been scared away were starting to come closer again. He could see them, about fifty meters back, staring and pointing at the ship. Well, so much for secretly coming aboard. They'd been spotted for sure.

Once they were inside the hatch, Scott palmed the lock on the opening to secure it. Short of bashing their way in, they weren't going to be able to come through there. Forcing the door was possible, but it was going to take them a long time. That thing was solid.

Of course, the dragon had been able to bite chunks out of the Stargazer, so it wasn't invulnerable. Just very strong. These people might still find a way to surprise him, which meant he needed to keep them on their toes instead.

"Toby, keep an eye on her. I'm going to work on a surprise for our other guests," Scott said.

He lowered himself back down to the control chair. As he'd expected, the whole gang was gathered around the base of the ship again. Two of them were dragging their sleeping buddy clear, but the other ten looked mad as hell and ready to do something about it. One of them started up the ladder, with another ready to climb right behind him.

"No, I don't think we're going to let you do that right now," Scott said.

The Stargazer had steering jets all around its nose to help with attitude control while in flight. They were designed to work in space, so they weren't incredibly powerful. But they ought to do the trick here.

"A little attitude control, coming right up!" Scott muttered as he fired up the steering thrusters.

Six jets around the nose cone ignited, sending bursts of hot gas outward from the ship. The men gathered jumped back. It looked like a couple of them were scalded. If they were, too bad. They were trying to attack his ship.

Hector was down on the ground in front of his cockpit window. Scott realized they could see him through the window. The chief was shaking his fist in Scott's direction and yelling something. Then three of his men tossed their spears at him.

They were good with those spears! All three smacked into the three-inch-thick transparent aluminum window. At least one of them managed to leave a scratch, too. Scott was impressed.

"I think they've backed off for the moment, but I'm sure they'll try something else again soon," Scott said. "Meanwhile, let's get our patient back for treatment."

"You take care of her. I'll watch the cameras to make sure your friends don't come up with new ways to play," Toby said.

"Sounds good," Scott said. "Speaking of which, how's my hearing doing?"

"I'm down to just above my normal volume now. Your hearing is recovering fine. A few more minutes and you'll be back to normal," Toby replied.

Well, that was a relief and a half. Now to make sure Tamara was OK, too. He led her by the hand up into the living quarters. Which was on its side, just like the rest of the ship. That was a pain in the neck, but he had to work with it for now. The autodoc was just a little further up the hull. Thank goodness there were plenty of handholds all over for moving about in zero gravity, otherwise the climb would be next to impossible.

He got Tamara up to the machine. It was a capsule with a lid that dropped down. She looked at it, then at him and frowned.

"I do not like the looks of this," she shouted.

Scott winced, then shouted back. "You don't have to be so loud!"

"Sorry," she replied in a quieter voice. "I can still barely hear."

"This device can fix that, but you need to go inside," Scott said.

"It's a device, not a cell? It looks like a prison."

"No. My sound blast hurt you. I just want to help fix the problem," Scott said.

Tamara nodded and climbed into the capsule. Scott tapped a few buttons on the screen and the lid slid shut over her. Another few buttons and the program activated. The first step was that the autodoc filled the capsule with a gas that would put her to sleep while it did its work. Tamara blinked a few times and then closed her eyes. Scott checked the vital sign monitors. She was unconscious, but otherwise fine. The machine would check her over and fix whatever it could.

He climbed back down to the cockpit to join Toby. The dog was staring out the window and watching various screens, each showing the feed from a different exterior camera.

"Anything new from our company?" Scott asked.

"Nope. They've all gathered over there," Toby said, nodding toward one screen. "They think they're being cunning by stepping out of view of the window. Like we can't watch them anyway."

"I doubt any of them have ever seen tech like this before. We need to give them a little leeway for not knowing how it works," Scott said.

"If we had a couple of guns mounted on the ship, I'd give them all the leeway they could ask for," Toby snarled.

Scott's eyebrows went up. "That's unusually blood-thirsty of you."

"I'm programmed to protect you, remember? That doesn't just mean saving you from yourself," Toby replied. "Hey, something's happening."

It was, indeed. The men who'd been gathered in a little cluster were moving. No, they were running! Fleeing back into the trees, dashing away from the ship as quickly as they could. It didn't make sense.

"We didn't do anything new. Why are they running away?" Scott asked.

As if in answer to his question, a massive roar echoed from somewhere above them.

EIGHTEEN

"Oh, shit."

It seemed like the understatement of the century, but damned if Scott could think of anything else to say. He knew what that roar had to be. There was only one critter he'd seen that could possibly be making that sort of noise from the air — unless this world had flying lions, too. He tapped the control panel, switching out one of the cameras to get a view of the air above.

The tail end of the Stargazer stuck out above the tree-tops. It wasn't much above them, but it had to be really damned obvious from the air. Plus they'd gone and made a bunch of noise with the high-decibel music. Oh, and then he'd fired the thrusters, too.

Of course all that activity had caught the attention of another dragon.

It was circling the ship, curious but not yet coming at them. Maybe it would decide the vessel was just a strange tree and move on. Scott held his breath, hoping. It would be so much easier if the big lizard just went elsewhere.

It stooped, the began a slow, circling glide down toward

the ship. As it came closer, Scott saw this one's wings glowing, just like the other one's had. They glowed more brightly as it came down. Was the glow related to their ability to fly? The first one he'd met had been in space. There wasn't any air to beat against there, so it had to be using something else for propulsion. Maybe it was the wings or something in the wings.

"Any suggestions?" Scott asked.

"Nope. I'm frozen in mortal terror," Toby replied. "Just kidding. I'm not programmed to feel mortal terror. An oversight, given who I was being assigned to."

"Thanks. Any helpful observations?"

"It's headed toward the main engine cup," Toby said.

It was indeed. The dragon set down on the edge of the massive cone that made up the back end of the Stargazer. Then it stepped down into the middle, and...

Scott couldn't see it anymore, but he had a bad feeling about this. There was a single camera inside the cone to monitor the output of the photon rocket engine. He flicked it on.

Yup, the dragon was curling up inside the cone. It folded its wings down around its sides, shifted its tail up so that it slipped over its eyes, and seemed like it was getting ready to bed down for the night.

"Aw. It looks like a cute little kitten," Scott said, beaming at the image. "This picture would have totally gone viral on Facebook."

"Yup. Except it looks like Facebook is long gone, and that cute little kitten is a couple tons of fang and claw with a bad attitude," Toby said.

"True, that," Scott said. He eyeballed the engine controls. "Luckily, I think we can get rid of it whenever we want. The photon rocket is basically a big laser."

"Yes," Toby said.

"Which the dragon is sitting on top of."

"Oh! That is good thinking. Well done, Scott," Toby replied, clearly impressed.

Scott smiled, feeling chuffed with himself. It wasn't every day Toby gave him a compliment. In fact, it almost never happened. His finger hovered over the button for a few moments. He could fire the engines up. That would definitely chase the dragon off. However, if the dragon left, they'd be dealing with the humans trying to break into the ship again. The dragon wasn't hurting anyone up there, and there was always the chance it would only be lightly singed by the laser. A sleeping dragon was better than a pissed-off dragon.

"I'm inclined to let sleeping dragons lie, at least for now," Scott said. "We can always zap it later if we need to."

"You're the boss," Toby said. "But that sounds like a good idea."

Scott leaned against the seat. He couldn't actually sit down, because the pilot's chair was facing directly toward the ground. That whole stabbing into the dirt thing was going to get annoying eventually. A problem for another day, though. Right then, he had the first relatively calm moment in quite a while. It was time to start thinking about what he should do next.

"This isn't the Earth we were planning on coming back to," Scott said.

"You're telling me? Where am I supposed to get WD-40 when we run out? My joints are going to be killing me before the year's over," Toby said.

"Lubricants are one issue. Food is another. But the whole point of taking this trip in the first place was to find my cure," Scott said. "The transmission we received from

Earth said it was at Berkeley. Which is a long-ass way away."

"With the ship, it's not too far. But there's no guarantee the university lab is still there," Toby said, echoing Scott's own fears.

"And the ship is facing entirely the wrong direction to lift off," Scott said. The main engine needed to be facing down, not up! Until it was, they weren't going anywhere.

Scott stared out the window at the forest as night slowly overtook the place. It looked like a woods from old Earth, if you ignored the fact that the trees were a hundred feet tall. Fireflies danced in the deepening dark, giving him an even greater sense of nostalgia. They had to figure out what had happened. Where were all the cities and people? How had everything fallen apart? Was there a war? And where had the dragons all come from?

He recalled the mystery planet he'd seen on approach. It was a good bet that had something to do with all the other problems. Was the arrival of a new planet enough to disrupt society completely? It would do damage, he was pretty sure of that. But take out everything? It seemed unlikely. It didn't explain the dragons, either. Bio-weapons in a final war?

"The stars are out," Toby said.

Scott glanced at the monitor the robot was watching. The stars were gorgeous. Without city lights to reduce their visibility, the whole Milky Way was spread across the sky in all its glory. He'd seen it this bright, but never in New England!

The vision calmed him, reminding Scott of camping trips with his father. They'd spent time out under the night sky together. His dad had shown him the constellations that were visible from each place they traveled. It was fun because there were so many different ones. Scott memorized all of them that he could. Even now, he could pick out a number of them from the screen.

"Scott, you remember I said we were a little off course?" Toby said.

Scott nodded. A meteor had damaged the ship while they were in transit. The damage had thrown off their thrust vector a ton. Scott repaired the damage, but they'd ended up accelerating more than intended. Instead of two hundred years passing on Earth, some number more had gone by.

"I've had the computer calculate the year, based on the star positions above and our rough longitude and latitude," Toby said. "Near as it can tell, we're not in 2256. We're not even close."

That was their target year. Scott already knew they'd overshot. But by how much? At this point, did it really matter?

"How bad is it?" Scott asked, when Toby didn't go on right away.

"We landed sometime around the year 2456. We over-shot our mark by about two hundred extra years."

NINETEEN

For a long moment Scott was frozen, barely able to think, let alone speak. Four hundred years in the future? Jumping forward two hundred had seemed a massive leap. But four? It was crazy. Earth should have been populated by a humanity that was as far ahead of the world he'd left behind as his era was beyond the middle ages. Maybe more, given the way technology had been advancing at a geometric rate.

Instead, he'd found humans living in warrens that were left over from the twenty-first century, using tech that was more reminiscent of the stone age, albeit with scraps of iron and steel. They'd probably gathered those from the ruins of his civilization, Scott realized.

Four hundred years. If he'd arrived at the correct year, would he have lived out his entire life before any of this happened? Would he have missed humanity's fall entirely? Or been there to watch it happen?

Instead, he was here to watch the scraps of what was still left, clinging to life even after all the lights had quite literally gone out.

Scott felt more tired than he'd been for a long time. In a way that was a good sign. Being able to sleep meant the FFI hadn't yet kicked into overdrive. His personal time-bomb was still ticking. But this exhaustion was more than just ordinary sleepiness.

"It's all gone, isn't it?" Scott asked.

Toby didn't answer at first. It was more or less a rhetorical question anyway, so Scott wasn't expecting much of an answer. He already knew. All he had to do was look out the window or check out the great bastion of society that was the cave-dwelling people who'd tried to imprison him within minutes of meeting him.

"It might be. Or it might not," Toby said at last. "We have the means to go and find out, if we work at it enough."

"The ship?" It didn't seem especially likely to ever fly again. They'd need to remove the nose from the ground and literally flip it end over end. The technology to accomplish that had existed when Scott departed Earth, but it would have been hard even in 2056. In 2456, it was beyond possibility.

"Humans made Stonehenge and the Great Pyramid with less technology than these people have," Toby reminded him.

That was true, but hadn't he heard once that archaeologists had tried to replicate those feats without success? No one could figure out how they'd done it. That didn't bode well for trying to lever a hundred-and-twenty foot spaceship into launch position.

"I just don't know what to do, now," Scott said. He kicked aimlessly at the chair. "I figured we'd have so much catching up to do when we landed that I'd spend the rest of my life learning about all the advances that had taken place while I was gone. And I could teach others, too, about how things had actually been in the twenty-first century."

Historians had a bad tendency to get the details wrong, in Scott's opinion. There always seemed to be things missing from the stories, and his best guess was that was the human element. People did things for reasons. Often, those reasons were more important than the actions themselves. But history tended to just recall the acts and not the motives behind them.

"You certainly have a lot you can teach here," Toby said.

Scott laughed. "Assuming they don't just drop me in a cell again?"

"You got out last time. I think you'll be even more prepared next time."

"You sound awfully confident there's going to be a next time," Scott said. "I'm not planning on getting captured again anytime soon."

Toby stared at him and make a strange sound from his speakers. It took Scott a moment to realize he was doing a dog-chuff version of laughter.

"What's so funny?" Scott asked.

"Knowing you, I think we can count on getting into trouble more often than not," Toby said, still laughing. But then he grew more serious and added another thought. "You do seem to be almost as adept at getting yourself back out of your predicaments as you are at getting into them, though."

Scott blinked. "Was that another compliment? That's what, two in one day? Three?"

"Don't push your luck," Toby growled. "Get some sleep. I'll watch the cameras and wake you if anything happens outside."

"OK," Scott said. He yawned cavernously. It had been

an exhausting morning. Even though the sun was still high overhead, a nap seemed like a good idea.

He made his way up from the cockpit into the next section. He peeked in on Tamara. She was still asleep, sealed in the pod as it treated her injuries. Scott smiled when he saw her. She looked so different asleep. The hard-ass warrior wasn't there anymore.

With luck, the pod would be able to repair her injuries. He felt guilty about that. It was his fault that she'd been hurt, his ship and its tech that had caused her eardrums to burst. The ship's medical systems were the best money could buy when he left. Would they be enough to heal her injuries?

Scott checked the readout. The prognosis looked good. His computer gave a high probability of Tamara recovering completely. That was a relief. Some good news at last.

His eyelids felt like they were growing heavier by the minute. Scott grabbed a blanket and slipped down to the lower wall, the one closest to the ground. Then he bedded himself down as best he could beneath a computer console. Tucked away like that, he felt secure. The cubby-like space felt comforting rather than confining.

Toby would remain alert to any problems. Scott knew he'd probably wake up to some other emergency soon enough, and that made it difficult for him to fall asleep right away. He was stuck between a rock and a hard place, here. Deadly dragon above and dangerous humans below.

Somehow he needed to figure out a way to resolve both issues safely. All while also getting his ship upright so that he could continue his journey.

None of which he had any idea how he was going to do.

"Well, it can't get any harder, at least," Scott murmured to himself.

He almost immediately regretted saying those words. Of course it could. Inviting Murphy over for a visit was never a good idea. In fact, with his luck, he had a bad feeling that not only could his situation get worse, it probably would.

Sleep took a long while to come, and when it did, Scott dreamt of dragons chasing him down dark tunnels.

TWENTY

"We've got a problem."

Toby's words snapped Scott awake. He sat up quickly. Too fast, in fact. His head collided against the console over his head with an echoing thud. He groaned and lay back down again.

"Are you all right? I felt that from up here," Toby asked.

Scott groaned a second time in response.

"Well, when you're finished banging your skull against the computer, our friends are back," Toby said.

Scott lifted his head again, careful this time to avoid smashing it into anything. He rose and clambered back down to the cockpit area. The new knot on his forehead joined the one from the day before on the back of his head. Scott touched the tender spot and winced. That was gonna leave a mark.

"What's going on?" Scott asked as he slid down the deck to the pilot's station.

A glance down at the monitor told him most of the story. The chief and his little band of tunnel dwellers were back. The threat of the dragon had kept them away for a while, but they were persistent. As he watched, they crept through the brush toward his ship.

"If they start banging on the hull again, there's going to be trouble," Toby said.

"Why?" Scott asked.

"Because our friend upstairs didn't leave. In fact, it looks like she's settling in to stay," Toby said.

"She?" Scott asked.

Toby tapped a monitor with a paw .The screen showed an image of the dragon still curled up in the rocket cone. But there was something new alongside the beast: three cat-sized oval orbs. They gleamed in reflected sunlight. Scott knew at once what they had to be.

The dragon had laid eggs on top of his ship.

"Unless males lay eggs in this species, it's a she," Toby said.

"Yeah, that could be a problem," Scott agreed.

The humans were almost to his ship. If they started trying to crack through the hull again, it would probably wake the dragon. Based on his interactions with the other dragon — the one now squashed beneath the nose of his ship — he didn't think that was going to go well for the humans. Mama dragon there was going to decide the humans looked like a tasty snack.

As irritated as Scott was at the chief for imprisoning him, he didn't think the man deserved to be eaten. After all, he was just trying to rescue his daughter.

"Oh shoot! Tamara!" He'd completely forgotten her in his rush to get down and see what was going on. She was still asleep in the medical pod.

Scott glanced at the screen again. Her people were still stalking their way toward the ship. Their movements were slow and cautious. Like they thought they could sneak up on him. They probably did think that, and to be fair, they had no understanding of the tech at his disposal. They didn't have heat and motion sensitive cameras like he did, and they probably wouldn't understand what they were even if he tried to explain them. But he knew someone who might be able to explain the danger they were headed into.

"I'm going to wake Tamara," Scott said. "She might be able to warn them off. They'll believe her, where they probably won't trust us."

"I'd suggest you hurry, then," Toby said.

Wishing again that he'd thought to arm the ship, Scott raced back to the handholds and started climbing up into the next ship section.

"Just one phaser bank and I could make most of my problems go away," he muttered, daydreaming about science fictional weaponry.

He'd figured that would be the sort of tech Earth would have when he returned. Nope, not even close. If the Stargazer represented the last significant technology still functioning on Earth, then it was a damned treasure trove for anyone who understood what it represented. The humans here would either fight over it or try to destroy it, once they understood it better.

Was there some way to go back in time? If he could just return the way he'd come, go back those extra two hundred years, then he could warn Earth what was coming. Maybe he could change the outcome.

Or maybe it was all locked. Scott shook his head. The ship wasn't a time machine. All he'd done was fly so fast that time swept by more rapidly for the rest of the universe. It was a one-way trip forward through time. He'd cast the dice, hoping to find a better world when he arrived.

Instead, he had this mess. He tapped the buttons on the

medical console a bit harder than he really had to. What was he going to do now? In the short term, Scott knew he'd simply been reacting to one crisis after another. Sooner or later, he needed to break out of that loop and work on longer-term planning. If he kept this up, eventually one of these emergencies was going to overwhelm him.

The medical pod opened, breaking into his thoughts. Tamara was still strapped down. Her limp body would have tumbled free from the pod otherwise. Scott tapped another command, and the system injected her with a stimulant to bring her back around. He'd have preferred to let her sleep it off. That was the safest, best bet. But her father didn't have time for that.

Tamara's eyelids fluttered. "What? Where am I?"

"In my ship. Remember? Your ears were hurt. I used my machines to help heal them. Can you hear me better now?" Scott said.

"Yes, I can hear you fine. Just a little dizzy," she replied.

"That should pass. Listen, I could use your help this time."

Tamara nodded. "Sure. What do you need?"

"Your father is outside. They were scared off for a bit, but they're coming back now," Scott said.

"I don't know if I can talk him out of attacking. Is your ship secure enough to hold them off?"

"Definitely. I don't think they can break in anytime soon," Scott said. "But that's not the problem. We need to stop them before they wake up the dragon sleeping on top of my ship and it decides they look like dinner."

TWENTY-ONE

B y the time Tamara and Scott got down to the cockpit, her father's team had managed to reach the ship. They were still being stealthy about their approach, thank god. If they'd already started banging on the door, it wouldn't have been pretty. Scott peered through the monitor, trying to figure out what they were up to. Two of the warriors kept watch while the other three and their chief were working with something on the ground.

"What are they doing?" Scott asked. He tapped the monitor to zoom the camera in, but the angle was still bad.

"At a guess, they're assembling a drill," Tamara said.

"You have drills?" Scott asked, his eyebrows shooting up.

"They're not hard to build from scraps of the old world, and they're essential to our survival. We've lost much, according to our records, but not everything."

Scott nodded absently. It figured that they'd have retained whatever they could of technology. He doubted they'd have a motor, but if they could power a drill by hand for long enough, it might well be able to rip through his hull.

A lot would depend on what quality alloy they used for the drill bit. The Stargazer was designed to take a beating, and Scott didn't think hand tools would be able to penetrate it easily.

"We need to stop them before they wake that up," Scott said, tapping the screen showing the sleeping dragon and her eggs.

"The laser might work as well," Toby reminded him.

"Or it might just wound the dragon and piss it off," Scott replied. "Tamara, can you let your father know about the danger?"

The cockpit was designed for one person. One person and a dog fit fairly well. Two people and a dog was getting overcrowded, and Scott was uncomfortably aware of how close she was to him. She seemed to be aware as well and took care to brush her arm against his as little as possible. He did the same out of respect for the woman, but her presence was... distracting. In a good way, he had to admit, but he could ill afford to lose his concentration just then.

"Can we speak to them with the device you used before? But with less volume?" Tamara asked.

"We could, but the speakers are set high enough on the ship that I worry anything loud enough for the men to hear it will also reach the dragon," Scott said.

"You're saying I have to go out there," Tamara said.

Scott nodded. "I'd do it, but I doubt your father would listen to me. He might listen to you."

Hell, half the reason Hector was still down there trying to break in was likely that the man's daughter was inside the Stargazer. If Scott had left her outside to fend for herself, he might have picked her up and taken her home, leaving him the hell alone. But then Tamara might have lost her hearing. Scott couldn't find it in himself to regret his decision.

"I'll do it. Show me how to exit?" Tamara asked.

"Of course. Toby, mind the screens?"

"Of course," the dog parroted back at him. Was it rolling its eyes?

There were a bunch of things on board the Stargazer that might be useful in this scenario, but most of them were back in the hold. He did have a few useful tools close at hand, though. Scott broke open the weapons locker in the main area and surveyed the handful of guns there. They had seemed like overkill back on Earth in 2056. But out here, in this mess? He found himself wishing he'd brought along a rocket launcher.

He slipped a .44 pistol from the rack and picked up a magazine for the weapon. Scott was proud that his hands didn't shake as he seated the rounds into the gun and pulled back the slide to chamber the first one. He'd never used a gun in violence. Never really thought he would ever need to. But he had enough hours on the range to know how to use all the weapons on board his ship.

Tamara stared at him as he clipped a holster to his belt and slid the pistol into it. She watched every move he made. Did she know what the weapon was? Scott didn't think it was likely any firearms had survived this long, and they certainly lacked the manufacturing capabilities here to make new ones. He didn't think she recognized it, but she might see the care he used in handling the gun and recognize it was a weapon.

Regardless, she didn't ask, and he didn't offer any information. With luck he wouldn't have to use the thing. If anything would wake up the dragon, gunshots would almost certainly do the trick.

Armed and ready, Scott led Tamara up to the airlock, then started it cycling. A quick glance at the monitors showed the coast was clear. Once he was sure there was no one outside waiting for them, Scott opened the interior door. He let Tamara slip in ahead of him, then followed her and closed the inner door. He held his hand over the palm-print reader, but before he pressed it and opened the door, he turned to Tamara.

"You helped me, back there. If this goes badly, try to get back into the ship. I can protect you in here," Scott said.

"And my people? My father?" she asked.

Scott frowned. How was he supposed to answer that? If he let them inside the ship, they'd have him and it. He wasn't about to just stand there and let them have everything.

"They imprisoned me," he replied.

"They were frightened. You are something new, and that scares people," Tamara said. "Give them time, and they will come to see you in a better light."

"Well, it probably couldn't get much worse than our initial introduction," Scott said with a chuckle.

"Oh, it could have. You might have been found by a Two-Chuck scouting party," Tamara said.

"Two-Chucks?" Scott asked. Then he shook his head. "Later. We're running out of time. Let's do this."

"I'll lead out," Tamara said.

Scott nodded and pressed his hand against the panel. The outer door hissed as it opened, letting the hot and humid air outside into the airlock. He was drenched in sweat within seconds. No wonder these people kept to lightweight clothing.

Tamara slipped out through the door, dropping down onto the nearest ladder rungs. Scott peeked out after her. Three of the men had already gathered around the bottom of the ladder. Two were gesturing at her to hurry down. The third had noticed Scott and raised his spear to throw it.

"There is a dragon," Tamara hissed, trying to whisper and pitch her voice to carry at the same time. "Be silent!"

But the men must not have heard her. The other two spotted Scott and raised their spears as well. He had one leg outside the ship because he'd been planning to follow Tamara down. One of the spears flew skyward, banging into the hull half a meter from his leg. Scott darted back into the airlock opening.

"Did that wake our friend?" Scott whispered into his comm unit.

"No, but she's shifting. Better hurry them out of there," Toby replied.

Scott peeked outside, curious but preferring caution to being turned into a kabob. Tamara was halfway down, gesturing with one hand for silence, but the men didn't seem to be getting her message. Finally her father stalked over to the base of the ladder. If anyone would understand the woman's desperate gesturing, it would be her father.

But he didn't. Instead, he stood at the base of the ladder, hands on his hips, and called up to her in a booming voice.

"Tamara, you are in a heap of trouble. Get down here this instant, girl! Move!"

The other men joined their chief in calling for her to climb down, even as she continued trying to hush them all. Scott groaned and leaned against the inside of the airlock.

"Status on our girl?" Scott asked over the radio.

"What do you think?" Toby replied.

A deafening roar came from somewhere above. Oh, yeah. The dragon was awake all right. Shit.

TWENTY-TWO

That had torn it. The dragon was awake. The entire ship shook as it rose and clambered up to the edge of the rocket cone. It shrieked rage at everyone in the vicinity. Scott clapped his hands over his ears. The dragon's call was more terrifying than anything he'd heard before.

The Stargazer shook again as the dragon lifted off. He could feel the wind from its wingbeats even inside the airlock. For those on the ground it must have been like getting caught in a sudden storm. And Tamara!

Scott peeked back outside. She clung to one of the ladder rungs, halfway between the hatch and the ground. The blasts of air buffeted her, but she gripped the rung with tenacity. She wasn't going to be knocked off easily.

The dragon was coming. He had to get her back inside the ship. Scott leaned outside. Tamara's eyes met his own.

"Come on! Climb up!" he called.

She shook her head and lowered herself down another rung toward the ground. Damn it, she wasn't going to retreat. Scott couldn't really blame her. If it had been his father at risk, would he have fled or tried to help? He knew the answer well enough.

Hector was in the center of a ring of his people. They stood around him, spears up, hopeless looks of fear on all their faces. They were in deep shit, and they knew it. The space beneath the high canopy of the trees was too open to hide. It was thick enough to screen the ground from the air pretty well, but if the dragon came down to ground level there would be precious few places left to hide.

They were all going to die, unless he did something.

Scott patted the pistol at his side to make sure it was still clipped there. He wasn't sure the weapon would do anything against as big a creature as the dragon, but at least it was a high enough caliber that it ought to feel the shots. Then he swung his body out of the airlock and down onto the top rung.

"God-damned-stupid-ass cave people," he muttered under his breath. "Don't know enough to keep quiet when a dragon is sleeping over their heads. No, they have to go wake the thing up. Then I have to go rescue their sorry asses..."

He kept up the steady litany as he descended the ladder. It was as much to keep his fear at bay as anything else. If he gave himself more than a few moments to think about what he was doing, Scott figured he'd be gibbering in terror.

A tearing noise that sounded like the entire world was coming apart at the seams drowned out all other sound. Leaves crackled and hissed, tree boughs shattered into splinters that flew everywhere. The shards pattered against the Stargazer's hull all around him. Scott clung to the rung, half expecting massive claws to drag him away.

But the dragon couldn't fly well below the canopy. Its

wingspan was too broad for flight on the ground. Instead, it crashed into the brush next to his ship. One of Hector's men was caught inside a massive front claw. He gave a brief cry and then was silent.

Scott winced and looked away. There was nothing else he could do for that one.

Then rest of Hector's men rattled their spears at the dragon as they backed away. It snorted at them. Then its head snapped out, snakelike in its speed, and grabbed one of their weapons in its teeth. The spear snapped in half instantly, the man holding it dragged from his feet. He tumbled forward to the ground.

The dragon didn't hesitate. It struck a second time, this time grabbing the fallen man in its fangs. He screamed as it lifted him up and away from the ground. The dragon shook him back and forth, biting down harder, but he was still alive.

"Tamara, we have to get back in the ship!" Scott called. There was nothing they could do against this monster. She was only a few rungs below him. If he could just reach her, drag her upward, maybe he could at least save her life from the beast.

The dragon was almost directly below them, still stalking closer to the remaining humans. It discarded the body of the man it had been holding in its teeth and snapped those massive jaws together again as it advanced.

Scott saw Tamara tense. Before he could ask her what she was doing, she dropped from the rung. He watched, helpless, as she plummeted the remaining feet toward the ground.

She landed square in the middle of the dragon's back. Scott saw her lash out with something. She was holding a knife! It rebounded from the dragon's scales the first time, but the second blow seemed to penetrate. The dragon thrashed about, trying to dislodge her. Tamara clung tightly to one of the creature's ridge spikes with one hand and her embedded dagger with the other, refusing to be bucked off.

It was time to put up or shut up. If Scott didn't do something fast, Tamara was done for. She could only hold on so long before the dragon shook her loose and ate her. He looped his left arm over the rung and drew his pistol.

Scott's hands were shaking. He used both to steady the weapon, aiming it down at the dragon. He had to be careful not to shoot Tamara, so aiming at the dragon's back was out of the question. Its head was another thing entirely, though. He took careful aim.

The pistol bucked as it fired, the sharp report reverberating through the forest. The round slammed into the ground next to the dragon's foreleg, churning up a big clod of dirt. The dragon noticed and turned its attention toward him. It roared, maw open toward Scott. He thought he was high enough to avoid its bite, but as he watched the neck continued rising. It was lifting its front legs from the ground to close the distance.

"No, you don't!" Scott yelled. He fired three more times, each report sounding like thunder. This time he didn't miss. The dragon roared and whipped its head away as the slugs slammed into its body.

It snapped the mouth shut, shaking its head in pain. Then it lunged upward again.

"Shit!" Scott shouted. He swung his body hard to the right, barely holding on to the ship with his left arm. The dragon's teeth snapped closed where he'd been standing a moment before.

Apparently a couple of bullets weren't going to be enough to do the job. Or at least, he'd have to hit something a lot more vital than he had so far. Scott turned the pistol and tried to aim at the dragon as its head reared back, but it was moving too swiftly to get off an accurate shot.

It roared again and took a step backward. Scott watched as the men lunged in with their spears, stabbing at the dragon's legs. He had to hand it to them, they had guts. He wasn't sure he could handle being down there with just a hand weapon. The dragon reached up with one large paw and swatted one of the men sideways. His body cracked into the ship's hull and slumped to the ground.

The others maintained their attack. They were backing the dragon up. Tamara continued hacking into its back, further enraging the animal. Swinging himself back onto the ladder, Scott took aim again. How many rounds had he fired? How many remained in the magazine? He hadn't counted, so he wasn't sure.

"Just need to make each one count," he said.

Squeeze the trigger gently, he reminded himself as he tried to slow his breathing enough to aim. The report startled him. The pistol bucked in his hand. He steadied his aim again and fired a second time. There were two splashes of blood on the dragon's neck where his rounds had entered its body.

It shrieked in pain and rage. But it must have decided this prey was more trouble than it was worth. The dragon beat its wings, blasting air back toward the men on the ground. The wind almost knocked Scott loose as well. He clung desperately to the ladder.

Three heavy wingbeats, and the dragon was airborne. It climbed up toward the canopy, turning as it rose. That was when Scott saw Tamara. She was still on the dragon's back, hanging on for dear life as it shot skyward through the trees and landed back on the rocket's cone far above.

TWENTY-THREE

S cott watched the dragon shoot upward through the trees, breaking out into the sky above. He half expected to see Tamara's body tumble down. Holding on through all that would be next to impossible. But she was made of stern stuff. Somehow, she managed to cling to the creature.

A rattling thud vibrating through the ship told Scott the dragon had landed back on its perch. He must have hurt it worse than he'd thought for it to retreat back to its nest. That was the good news — his weapons could do some damage. He'd been half afraid that even the hardest hitting weapons he had available wouldn't be enough to damage the dragon. Clearly he could hurt it, and he'd already seen firsthand that they could be killed.

Killing this one might be a little harder, but he wasn't sure there would be any other way to rescue Tamara. If she could be saved at all.

"Toby, you've got eyes on the dragon?" Scott asked over the radio.

"Affirmative. It has returned to its eggs. The woman is still on its back."

Still? How the hell was she managing to hold on? That wouldn't last. The dragon had plenty of space up there to knock her off.

"It's rolling over," Toby said. "She dove off."

He felt helpless down there. Even if he started climbing now, by the time he got up to the top of the ship it would all be over. If Tamara was going to survive it would be up to her.

"Smart woman. It tried to bite her, but she used one of the eggs for cover. The dragon is being careful around its eggs," Toby said. "Now she's slipping into the laser apparatus. It can't reach her there, although it's trying to claw its way in."

"It'll probably manage, if it has enough time," Scott said, recalling how the first dragon had chewed chunks out of his ship.

"Probably. She has at least a few minutes, if she's careful."

Not much time to mount a rescue. Scott holstered the pistol and looked up. He had a lot of climbing to do if he was going to get up there and help. First he'd better get more ammunition. He had a feeling he was going to need it.

A spear slammed into the hull just next to his fingers as he reached up to climb. Startled, Scott lost his grip on the ship. He tried vainly to grab hold again but tumbled backward toward the ground.

The impact knocked all the air from his lungs. He rolled over, gasping for breath. At least he hadn't blacked out this time. His shoulder hurt like hell from the fall, though. Scott glanced up and saw a trio of spears leveled at his head.

"You have got to be kidding me," Scott said.

"This is your fault," Hector growled, stepping between his men. "Tamara is dead. Now you will join her!"

Scott wanted to reason with Hector. Wanted to tell him that his daughter was still alive. That he was trying to rescue her. But the look on Hector's face was pure rage. Scott didn't think he was going to be able to reason with the man.

Hector snatched a spear from one of his men and took a step forward, raising the weapon to strike.

Scott launched himself back to his feet, half-stumbling backward as he rose. He pulled the pistol loose from its holster as he stood. Damn it, he didn't want to kill these people, but it was fast looking like they weren't going to give him much choice. Still, maybe he could convince them to at least stop and listen to him.

He fired the pistol. The crack of its report made two of the men jump back. The round struck the ground between Hector's feet, splashing dirt all over his legs. He stopped moving and eyed Scott warily.

"A weapon?" Hector asked.

"Yes. The same one I used to drive the dragon off," Scott replied.

"With my daughter," Hector snarled.

"She's alive, Hector. But she doesn't have much time," Scott said.

"How can she be alive? The dragon took her!"

Scott held the pistol steady with his right hand and reached into his pocket with the other, pulling out a small tablet.

"Toby, route the rocket camera to my device, please," Scott said.

"Done," the dog replied.

The tablet screen lit up, showing Tamara huddled

beneath the struts supporting the massive cone. She was practically on top of the photon drive itself. Scott winced. That had been their ace in the hole, the one weapon he was pretty sure would fry the dragon instantly. But he couldn't fire up the drive with Tamara in there. She'd cook even more quickly than the big lizard would.

Scott turned the display around so Hector could see his daughter. He shook as he watched her hide from the teeth still trying to gnaw their way down to her. The spear dropped from his hands.

"How can you do this? What sort of device shows you her image?" Hector asked.

"It's a camera," Scott said. He sighed. These people had no inkling of technology beyond the basics. Had humanity lost everything? "Once, almost everyone had one of these in their pocket."

"Not in my lifetime," Hector replied.

"Not in many lifetimes. Listen, I can explain more. But Tamara is running out of time."

"How can I help?" the chief asked.

Thank god. Now that he'd seen his daughter alive and fighting to stay that way, Hector was on board. That improved their odds of saving her life from virtually no prayer to maybe having a snowball's chance in hell.

"We're going to need to get the dragon away from her. Once it's distracted elsewhere, someone has to go in there and help her out," Scott said.

Hector's men glanced at their feet. Scott wanted to chuckle, but held it back. The dragon was scary enough for him to face, and at least Scott had the benefit of watching movies about people killing the damned things. It made it easier to imagine himself in the starring role of some sort of motion picture.

But if what he'd heard was right, none of these people had ever killed a dragon or even heard of one being killed by a human. These creatures were the ultimate boogeymen for them, brutal killers that they were helpless to defend themselves against.

Well, they weren't helpless anymore. Scott had weapons that could put a dent in even a dragon. It was time to put them to use.

"Are you with me, Hector? I need to go, whether you're coming or not. She's almost out of time," Scott said.

"You would try to rescue her regardless of whether I come or not?"

"Of course. She helped me," Scott said. "She's my friend. I'm not letting her down now."

The chief snapped him a sharp nod. "A man of honor. I will come with you, Scott Free. Assuming we survive, I will owe you a great debt."

Hector reached out a hand. Scott held out his own, and the two men shook hands in a gesture of friendship that had survived in spite of all humanity's troubles.

TWENTY-FOUR

The climb back up the ladder hurt less than how he'd gotten down, but sore as Scott was it was still a painful ascension. He wasn't looking forward to the second half of the climb. At least he'd gotten back to the airlock door. Now, how to get back inside to grab some more ammunition without giving Hector a close-up of the inside of his ship?

They were on the same side, for now. But he wasn't willing to just forget that the man had imprisoned him just the day before. Allies of convenience were just that. As soon as it became less convenient, Scott knew he might find himself back in a cell again. Better to keep some secrets to himself.

"Brought you a few things you might need," Toby's voice said from just above his head.

Scott jumped and almost lost his grip on the ladder again. "Toby! Don't surprise me like that!"

"Sorry. Not sorry," the dog said, chuckling. "Thought you could use some additional firepower. Brought you more rounds for the .44 and the biggest bore rifle we have on the ship."

"It speaks?" Hector asked from a few feet below.

"Woof?" Toby barked.

"I think the cat is out of the bag. Or dog, as the case might be," Scott said. "Yeah, he talks. He's also a pain in the neck when he wants to be, Hector. Trust me."

Hector laughed. "You are showing me many new things. I suspect you have even more to demonstrate, once we have my daughter back. Is she still well?"

"She's still hidden in the engine, if that's what you mean by well," Toby replied. "But the dragon is doing a number on our drive systems."

"We'll put a stop to that," Scott said.

He took the rifle from the airlock deck and slung it over his back. The thing was massive, with a scope on the top. What caliber was it? He didn't remember. It would say, somewhere on the ship's manifest. Anyway, a bigger bore meant bigger holes in the dragon. Probably.

He slipped out the magazine from his pistol and replaced it with a fresh one. Shit, he'd been down to just two bullets. It's a good thing the chief hadn't decided to attack anyway. He might have nailed one or two of the men before they poked him full of holes with their spears. Had to remember to bring more than one magazine from now on.

What a crazy world. Scott had never imagined needing to defend himself like this. Well, that was why he had the weapons on board. In case he ran into trouble when he got back to Earth. But never in a million years had he really expected to use them!

"Time to climb some more," Scott said. "You ready to roll?"

"I am ready," Hector replied.

"Secure the ship," Scott told Toby. "Nobody comes in but me."

"Aye, Captain! Shall I swab the decks for you, too, sir?"

"Just... argh. See what I mean, Hector?" Scott said. "Make the ship as secure as you can and be ready to fire up the drive if I order it."

Toby stilled. "With you up there?"

"I hope it won't come to that, but be ready no matter what," Scott said.

"Gotcha. I'm off," Toby said. The outer hatch slid closed.

"A remarkable beast," Hector said. "Where did you acquire him?"

"A gift from my mom," Scott replied.

"You must have a remarkable mother."

"You don't know the half of it," Scott laughed. "Come on, still a ways to go."

He led the climb up the side of the ship. It was a long way up. Damn, but his arms were getting tired. The last part of the climb was going to be the worst, too. The rungs clung close to the hull all the way. That meant when it came to climbing the rungs attached to the rocket cone, they were going to be ascending what amounted to an overhang.

That was going to suck.

Scott halted just before the cone. He looped his arms through the rung so he could take the weight off them and shook out his hands. His shoulders burned. His wrists weren't much better, and his hands were shaking.

"Are you all right? Why did we stop?" Hector asked.

"Just need to catch my breath," Scott replied.

Hector didn't seem to have half the problems he was. But then Hector looked like he was built of solid muscle. He had to be five or six inches taller than Scott and fifty pounds heavier. None of that extra weight was fat, either.

Adding insult to injury, the big man had his spear strapped across his back with some sort of fancy rope sling. It was twice as long as Scott's rifle, and it was all he could do to keep the gun from tangling him up as he climbed. Hector didn't seem to have any problems, though.

"We must hurry," Hector said.

"It's not going to get us to the top more quickly if I fall off," Scott snapped.

"Ah. I see," Hector said. He looked thoughtful for a moment, scanning the way above. Then he slipped his spear free from his back, carefully unwinding the rope which held it there.

He lowered the spear down and trapped it with his knees. Holding the rung with one hand, he somehow unraveled the sling into a length of rope. He held that out to Scott.

"Take it. Tie yourself in," he said. "If you fall, at least it won't be the entire way."

"What about you?" Scott asked as he took the rope.

"I will make the climb. My daughter's life depends on me."

Good enough, Scott figured. He tied the rope off to the rung above him and then to a loop at belt level on his shipsuit. It was designed to hold his weight. It ought to work here.

That done, Scott took a deep breath and began ascending again. Now the way was much harder. Each new rung brought him further away from the center of the ship as the cone angled away. His feet slipped from a rung, leaving him hanging by his hands, his legs pinwheeling in the air.

Scott looked down and regretted it at once. That fall was going to suck, even if he only fell partway. Assuming the rope and clip held. There was no guarantee they would. He was over a hundred feet up. What the hell was he doing out there? He was no action hero! This was real life, not a game. He could die out there.

"Scott. Listen to me," Hector said. His voice was soft. "I know what you are thinking. I have been there too. Fear lives in all of us. You have shown yourself willing to fight through that fear, which makes you the best kind of man. You can do this."

Pulling with all his strength, Scott lifted his feet back to the ladder rungs. The person who's designed this system was a damned sadist. Well, maybe not. The Stargazer was upside-down, after all. This should have been the easiest part of the climb, instead of the hardest. He reached for the next rung and lifted himself up.

Damned if he was going to let chief know-it-all show him up. Face his fear? Overcome it? Ha!

"I live with fear every damned day of my life," Scott said between gritted teeth. "I have been overcoming it for years now. This? This is nothing."

He lifted himself up another rung, not sure if he'd been speaking to Hector or himself. Whichever it had been, the words seemed to work. New energy flowed through exhausted limbs. He was almost to the end of the ladder. Another rung. Just a few more and he would be at the top.

Tamara needed him. She'd come through for him when he was imprisoned. She even went against her own father and chief to help him get out. Now she was in trouble, and he was the most likely rescue team. Not like Hector was going to get far with his spear against a dragon. It might use the weapon as a toothpick after it was done eating him.

The thought made Scott grin. He didn't actually want to see Hector eaten, but it would be nice to see him get a little of his own back. The irony of teaming up with the guy who'd knocked him out yesterday to fight a monster that could kill them both with a twitch of its tail wasn't lost on him.

Scott reached up for another rung and found there were no more. He pulled himself slowly over the edge of the cone, straddling it with his legs, and peered down.

TWENTY-FIVE

The dragon was facing away from him. That was a relief. He hadn't thought over what to do if the dragon happened to look up as he clambered over the edge. That might have resulted in the shortest-lived rescue mission of all time.

It was down at the base of the cone, facing in toward the drive. The creature had something in its teeth — her teeth, Scott reminded himself. This dragon was a mom.

The eggs were near her, resting against what was left of the photon drive's external apparatus. Scott winced. The 3D printer on board the ship could replace those parts, but it would take a while. The drive might still fire right now, but it could also blow off the back end of the ship. Hard to say which would happen.

The stuff in the dragon's teeth were bits of his ship. As Scott watched, it spat out a chunk of metal and then leaned down again to chew out another section.

OK, that was about enough. The Stargazer was his, and the last thing Scott wanted was to watch some oversized lizard chew it up.

"How do we proceed?" Hector asked, keeping his voice soft.

He'd climbed up beside Scott so silently that he hadn't heard the chief arrive. That was good, given that they really didn't want to attract any unnecessary attention. The man still had his spear! Scott looked down at the rope still tied to his suit. How had he hauled that up without the sling?

"One of us needs to distract it while the other climbs down to rescue Tamara," Scott whispered. He untied the rope. It was long enough to drape down a little ways into the cone. It would give them something to climb out with.

But the airlock was a long way down. How they were going to get there without the dragon picking them off the side of the ship, Scott didn't know. One step at a time.

"I can get its attention quickly enough. These dragons care for their young as we do," Hector said. He raised his spear over his head.

Before Scott could say a word, Hector hurled the spear. It slashed through the air. Scott couldn't see how the simple weapon would do more than bounce off the dragon's scales, but the mother wasn't Hector's target.

The spear struck one shimmering egg and shattered it. Scott was expecting something like a bird's egg, all runny goo flowing everywhere. But the inside of the egg was mostly dry. The spear had punched through the outer shell and stabbed into the small dragon inside. It cried out once, a high-pitched yowl. Then it was silent.

Mama dragon was not. She whirled at the sound of her egg shattering and moved her body to cover the eggs. Scott saw her sniffing the dead baby dragon. Then her head darted up glancing around to look for threats. Her eyes locked on Hector and Scott, and she roared.

Dragon breath stank. Scott got a clear whiff from where

he was sitting, which he decided was way too close to a man-eating lizard for his personal comfort.

He whipped the pistol up from its holster and aimed. Meanwhile, Hector leaned forward and slid down the inside of the cone. The dragon tried watching both of them, but decided Hector was the more immediate threat. He was the one moving closer to her eggs, after all. Her head darted toward him, maw open.

Scott fired. He unloaded the entire magazine into the dragon's head and neck. She screamed in a shrill tone and backed away, moving up the opposite side of the cone. The dragon was hurting, but she wasn't out of the fight yet. He pressed the button to drop the magazine. It went clattering down the cone as he loaded a second one.

Hector had snatched his spear back up and was yelling something to Tamara. She hollered back, but Scott couldn't hear their words over his ringing ears. The damned pistol was loud. He had the new magazine loaded and aimed it back at the dragon. It was just in time. She was already moving back toward the center where Hector stood. Scott took aim and pulled the trigger.

The pistol clicked but didn't go off. What was wrong? Shit, he'd forgotten to pull back the slide and load the first cartridge! He reached up and worked the action on the pistol, then aimed it again.

The dragon was already danger-close to Hector. Scott couldn't shoot without risking a hit to the man instead of the monster. He shifted his aim to her body and squeezed off a shot, but wasn't even sure if he'd hit.

Hector stabbed out with his spear. The dragon snapped back at him. It roared, then let loose with a burst of flame, but he dove sideways just in time. Scott managed to nail the dragon with two more shots, but then it whipped its tail around, sweeping Hector's legs out from under him. The crack of bones snapping was louder than the chief's screams.

He rolled away from the dragon. Scott knew the man had to be in incredible pain, but he kept fighting anyway. He'd dropped his spear, but was reaching for something on the hull.

Then Hector rolled over onto his back and presented one of the other eggs to the dragon. She had been closing in to finish him off but halted when she saw the egg in danger. The dragon let out a hiss as it slowly leaned in.

"Get out of there!" Hector shouted to Tamara.

"Not without you!" she cried.

"Go now!"

She shook her head. The woman was being as stubborn as her father. Damned if Scott wasn't going to have to figure out a way to save the both of them. He holstered the pistol and unslung the rifle from his shoulder. It had to have more punch than the little gun. He hoped it did, anyway. He needed something that would do more than sting the dragon.

Then he grabbed the rope and swung himself down into the cone. He stumbled a bit coming to a stop, but at least now he had a better angle from which to aim at the dragon.

"Hey, you!" Scott shouted.

The dragon turned toward him and let out an angry hiss. Well, he had its attention now, anyway. Time to see what he could do about it. Scott drew the rifle up to his shoulder and aimed at the dragon's chest. She started moving toward him, opening up her belly as a perfect target. Scott squeezed the trigger.

The recoil sent him back on his tail and almost tore the rifle from his hands. He'd never fired a gun that hit like that!

Echoes of the shot rang in Scott's ears. He shook his head, trying to clear it, and raised the rifle to his bruised shoulder again.

The dragon was still coming toward him, but it was staggering with each step. Blood poured from a fist-sized hole in her chest. Her eyes were full of pain and fury. The dragon knew she was hurt badly, probably dying. But she would do everything in her power to take down the man who'd hurt her before she went.

Scott squeezed the trigger a second time. This time, he was better braced against the recoil. He still felt like the hammer-blow of the stock had shattered his collarbone, and his entire right arm went numb. But he stayed on target and was able to fire a third shot.

The impacts slammed into the dragon. She reared back after the first, roaring. Then the second struck. She tumbled over backward and was still.

Silence was everywhere. At least, as far as Scott could tell it was. He couldn't hear a damned thing over the ringing in his ears. He slung the rifle over his shoulder and limped to Tamara so he could help her out of the hollow spot she'd hidden in.

She raced to her father's side. Scott saw the chief moving, and figured he was fine for the moment. He went over to the dragon's head. Better to make sure it was actually dead. No sense taking any chances.

But her eyes were already glazing over in death. She was gone. A tear rolled down Scott's cheek. He couldn't help but feel sad. Sure, it was a murderous killing machine, but it was also a mother trying to fend for her young.

He reached down and patted the dragon's nose, feeling her rough scales under his hand.

"I'm sorry," Scott whispered. "I was just trying to

defend people who matter to me. Same as you. I wish it could have been different."

One of the eggs was shattered under her head. The baby inside had been crushed when she fell. More senseless death, for no reason. Scott felt anger broiling inside his chest. He wanted to put a stop to the stupid violence. How, he didn't know. But he would find a way.

The third egg still rested on the hull nearby Hector. He'd let go of it and it had rolled away. Scott leaned down and examined the egg. It seemed intact.

Careful not to damage it, he rolled it down into the hollow spot where Tamara had been. He could recover the egg later. Maybe he couldn't find a way to save Tamara without killing its mother and siblings, but he could save this one. If he was going to find a way to end the fighting, he had to start somewhere.

TWENTY-SIX

Getting Hector down turned out to be simpler than Scott had feared. His people climbed up and rigged ropes to the top of the cone. They laid their chief gently into a litter and prepared to slowly lower him back to the ground.

Despite the victory and rescue, the mood was somber. Hector had shattered bones in both legs. The damage was pretty extensive. Scott's doc-in-a-pod might be able to do something with injuries that severe, but without proper medical attention it was uncertain whether the man would ever walk again.

Scott took Tamara aside to ask her what she thought. It was her father, after all. She'd already seen the pod. Keeping that a secret wasn't in the cards anymore. But letting Hector into the Stargazer meant trusting the man with a lot more secrets. Scott wasn't certain he was ready to do that yet.

"You can fix him, yes? The way you fixed me?" Tamara asked, touching her ears.

"I think so. His injuries are severe, but the pod can at least help him along the way toward recovery," Scott said.

Tamara sensed his hesitation. She tilted her head like she was listening. "But you don't know if you can trust us. I can appreciate that."

"He did hit me over the head and lock me up," Scott pointed out.

"He did. But now you and he are allies. How better to cement that alliance than for you to offer him something as a gift?" she asked. "My father is an honorable man, Scott. If you cannot trust him, can you trust my word on that?"

Tamara had been true every step of the way. He hadn't hesitated to bring her inside the ship when she was hurt. Was it just because she was a woman? Scott liked to think he was immune to that sort of sexist behavior. His mother would have run him over with a truck.

No, the truth was he did trust her. He had trusted her instinctively since they first met. Her father had yet to show enough reason for that sort of trust, but Tamara already had. If she vouched for her father, it had to be good enough for him as well.

"We'll do it, then. Let's see if we can convince him," Scott said.

"To get a look inside your ship at all your wonders? I don't think that will be as hard as you think," Tamara replied.

"You're probably right," Scott said.

He walked over to the chief, still laying on the litter as his men prepared to hook it up to ropes and lower him down. Hector's face was drawn and pale, but he was still alert. The pain had to be incredible, but he never cried out as the litter jostled about. The man was impressive. Scott thought he would have been crying like a little baby.

How to deal with someone like that? In some ways, Hector felt like every jock Scott had ever run into. Big, strong, easily comfortable with his body. Tall, handsome, able to get his own way easily. But there was more to the man than that. He'd risked his life to save his daughter. Moreover, he had charged a dragon head-on, trusting Scott to finish the job if he fell in battle.

That had to count for something, right? Scott crouched down beside his litter.

"Thank you, my friend," Hector said, reaching out to clasp Scott's hand. "Thanks to you, my daughter is safe again. And you've shown she was right. You are indeed a slayer of dragons."

Scott chuckled. "The first one was something of an accident. It attacked me."

"But the second?" Hector asked, a small smile on his lips.

"I almost peed my pants," Scott said.

"You stood your ground like few men would have. Don't demean your efforts with self-disparagement. It does not become men like us."

"If you say so," Scott said. He didn't feel like he was anything near Hector's class. He'd had guns. Hector stood the dragon down with a spear and deliberately drew the beast's attention to buy Scott time.

"Listen," Scott went on, hoping to change the subject. "Your legs are badly hurt."

"Are they? I hadn't noticed," Hector said. He tried to shift his right leg and winced, drawing a sharp breath.

"I might be able to help you recover more quickly," Scott said.

"Oh? More of your powers, like the weapons you carry?" Hector asked.

They'd never seen a gun before. No wonder they'd backed down when he showed it off on the ground. They had no idea what it was, what it could do. But they'd seen it kill a dragon, now. They might not understand technology, but Scott had shown them enough to believe in its power.

"Something like that. But you'll have to come inside my ship. You'll also sleep, for a few hours at least. Maybe as much as a day."

"You would invite me inside the cavern of wonders? What are my odds of ever returning, once I enter this strange ship of yours?" Hector asked. Then he waved away his own suggestion. "No, my daughter has already come forth. She told me you used this healing magic on her. I am grateful for you offering it to me. I have seen wounds like mine before. They rarely end well."

"It's not magic," Scott said.

"Can I do those things you do?" Hector asked.

How truthful should he be? If Hector understood that the gun was a simple tool that anyone could carry, would he try to take them away? Once he knew the ship was just a collection of such devices, would he ever let Scott go away in his vessel? He had a feeling he might end up stuck there a long time. Time was the one thing he most definitely did not have on his side.

"No, not easily. Perhaps in time I could teach you some of it, though," Scott said.

"I would appreciate any teaching you can do," Hector replied. "For now, I will take what gifts of health you are able to bestow. I will order my men to follow my daughter's lead while I am gone, and to return to me tomorrow. At high-sun?"

Scott did a little mental math. "That should be enough time, yes."

"Good. Then if you will show me the way into your ship?" Hector said.

Getting him down wasn't difficult. Many hands made for light work, and these people understood pulley systems very well. Scott went down ahead to open the hatch and pull the chief inside once he was at the airlock.

Then Tamara and another man descended to help him carry Hector inside and get him up to the medical pod. That was harder than coming down had been. Having the ship sitting on its nose was becoming a pain in the neck. He needed to solve that issue and soon. Hector noticed the strange layout.

"It seems like your ship is not upright as it should be," he said.

"It's not. It's nose down right now," Scott admitted.

"Perhaps when I wake we can help you with that," Hector replied.

"That would be terrific. Got any hydraulic lifts? Cranes?" Scott asked. He wasn't feeling much confidence in their ability to flip the ship using stone-age tech.

"We might surprise you yet," Hector said.

Then the pod slid shut. There was a hissing sound as it administered a sleeping agent to the chief, who went under almost immediately. The guard jumped at the sight.

"Relax; he's just sleeping. He'll be much better when he wakes," Scott said.

The man looked at Tamara, who nodded. Only then did he begin to calm down again. She hurried him back to the airlock. Scott was glad for her help. No sense leaving him nearby to add to his unease when he saw the pod start working on those injuries.

"Tomorrow then, Scott?" Tamara asked in the airlock doorway.

"Tomorrow. And thank you for your help," Scott said.

"Thank you. You and my father saved my life," she replied. "I won't soon forget that."

Then she descended the ladder, rejoined her people, and started down the path toward her home. Scott shook his head as he sealed the hatch shut.

"What's bugging you?" Toby asked.

Scott jumped. "Don't startle me like that!"

"Woof. It's what I do, boss," Toby replied. "But why the long look? You killed the monster and saved the girl. You're a hero. Congrats."

"It's not that simple," Scott said.

Nothing was simple here. The world he'd grown up in was gone. He'd been looking forward to seeing what the future had in store, but now that he'd seen it, Scott felt like he had the world's worst case of buyer's remorse ever.

TWENTY-SEVEN

There was one more thing he needed to do before resting, though. Scott popped the airlock open again.

"Need your help for a minute," he said.

"With what?" Toby asked.

"Just pull the thing I lower down inside the hatch," Scott said.

Then he climbed back to the rocket cone and fetched the egg he'd hidden there. It's mother's body still sat there, slowly starting to stink in the sunlight. He needed to get rid of the thing. It was going to be truly repugnant in a few days.

Scott carefully tied ropes to the egg and then lowered it down. Once it was level with the airlock, he called down to Toby on his radio.

"Haul it in, please. I'll be right down."

"Is that what I think it is?" Toby asked.

"You know perfectly well what it is," Scott replied.

"Yup. Just making small talk. Maybe not the best idea, bringing a dragon into the ship?"

"It's not a dragon. It's a dragon egg," Scott replied.

"I'm not sure the distinction matters once it hatches, and this egg looks close," Toby replied.

"How can it be close to hatching? Didn't she just lay those eggs less than twenty-four hours ago?" Scott asked.

"Do not meddle in the gestational periods of dragons, for you are crunchy and taste good with ketchup," Toby replied. "I can't tell you why it happened so fast, but this egg looks almost ready to pop, to me."

"Well, shit," Scott said.

He'd hoped to have some time to study the thing before it hatched, but it didn't seem like they were going to have much leeway. He recalled how the egg Hector split with his spear hadn't spilled out runny fluid. Instead there'd been a mostly-formed baby dragon inside. Maybe the eggs were mostly ready to hatch before the mom laid them? That would be a strange way for a species to operate, but it wasn't impossible to imagine.

Scott looked over at the mother dragon's body. He could learn a lot more from her, but he didn't have the stomach for dissection. Tablet photos would have to do. He snapped a bunch. Then he recalled one facet of the dragon's anatomy which was particularly interesting.

Those wings were just way too small to hold up a creature so massive. Plus, he'd seen one flying in space, without air. Clearly they weren't just using wingbeats to remain aloft.

Every time he'd seen a dragon aloft, the wings glowed. They were dark now, but he'd seen the ribbing of each wing glow before. Especially in space, but Scott had noticed it when this one took off with Tamara, too. Why the glow? Was it related in some way to their flight?

Resolved to check it out, Scott pulled out a knife from

his belt. He went over to the wing and cut into the leathery stuff. It came apart easily enough, but as soon as he hit the rib his knife stopped cold.

Scott sawed at the material for another minute, trying to cut through it. He had a hard time telling what it was made of through the blood and goo dripping from the wings. The slime was making his hands slippery, and he had to be careful not to slice himself with his own knife.

It wasn't cutting. If anything, the stuff was actually dulling his knife. Scott shook his head. Maybe a bolt cutter could get him a sample, but he was utterly spent. Climbing back down to the ship was going to be difficult enough. Coming back up with cutters, then back down again afterward? It wasn't happening. Not today, anyway.

He dropped the wing and stood back up. The goop from the wings was all over his hands. That wasn't going to make climbing down easier. He looked around for something to wipe it off on, didn't see any obvious answers, and gave up his already messed up ship-suit as a lost cause, wiping the slime off on it.

Then he climbed back down to the airlock. It took all his energy to get inside and close up the ship. He peeked in on Hector. The pod was starting to work on his legs. It was not a process for the squeamish to watch. Scott glanced in, curious, then looked away after less than a minute.

"So that's what bone looks like," he said. "Gross."

He tapped the console and made sure the pod would keep Hector under until just before noon. It trilled an affirmative response and continued working on its patient.

"What are you planning to do with our little guest?" Toby asked.

"He's secure in the pod," Scott said, thinking the dog was talking about Hector.

"No, I don't mean the big guest. I'm talking about the small one," Toby said. He tapped the egg meaningfully with his nose.

"Oh, right! Um. I'd love to put it in the pod to get a full medical scan, but it's occupied," Scott said. "I guess we just do the best we can with what we've got."

He hoisted the egg up onto a table and proceeded to scan the thing with every device he could grab. Oddly, nothing he had seemed able to penetrate the shell. It was almost completely impervious to every wavelength of EM radiation he could throw at it.

"Weird stuff," Scott said. His eyelids were getting heavy. How long had he been up?

He rapped the egg with his knuckles.

Was that a tapping he felt back against his hand?

Scott kept his palm against the thing for about a minute, but there were no more taps. It must have been his imagination.

"I'll lay my head down for a few minutes," Scott said. "Just a short rest, then I can work on it again."

He cradled his head in his arms and fell fast asleep in minutes.

On the table in front of him, the egg began to rock back and forth.

TOBY WAS WASHING HIS FACE. That didn't make sense. Toby was a robot. He didn't have a tongue. But Scott's face was getting washed, and he could hear Toby talking to him. What the heck was going on?

Scott's eyes snapped open, taking in the scene in front of him. Eggshell fragments littered the table, and a winged lizard the size of a medium dog sat on his lap, gently washing his face with a raspy tongue.

"Eww!" Scott said.

"Mrrrp?" the dragon replied.

Scott was nervous about making sudden moves. The hatchling had popped out while he was napping. Beautiful. So much for doing any more research on the egg.

He reached down to his belt, where the pistol was still holstered. If this dragon thought he was going to be a quick lunch, it wasn't going to happen.

The dragon leaned in again, the head moving with snakelike speed directly at his face. Scott didn't even have time to cry out.

Its tongue slurped up his whole face, from chin to forehead. Then the dragon sat back and chirped at him.

"Made a new friend, oh mother of dragons?" Toby asked.

"How long have you been standing there?"

"Long enough to see that lizard give you a much-needed bath. I can't say I disagree with its sense of hygiene."

"How long since it hatched, you electronic annoyance?" Scott asked.

"Less than ten minutes ago. I came as soon as the monitor told me it was busting out. But it didn't look like it was hurting anything," Toby said. "And like I said, you needed that bath."

Scott gently pushed the hatchling back onto the table and stood up. He took a step away from the table. It stared up at him expectantly. He backed up one more step. It chirped, then hopped off the table and walked up to nestle itself between his legs.

"Looks like you're the mommy now," Toby said. "Good

luck figuring this one out. I told you it was going to hatch soon. Now what are you going to do with it?"

Scott reached down and scooped the little dragon up. He scratched it under the chin, and it cooed at him. Still holding the dragon cradled in one arm, he made his way to the galley cabinets and fished around, looking for something a dragon might enjoy eating.

"You want to try hot dogs? Do those sound yummy?" Scott asked.

"Mrrp?"

Taking that as an affirmative, Scott opened up the package and fished around inside for one. He slipped it out and held it out to the dragon. It took two quick sniffs of the hot dog and then gulped it down whole.

"Mrrp!" it said, staring at the rest of the package.

"Hungry, are we?" Scott said, laughing. "OK, I'll get you another."

"Oh, we're feeding wayward man-eating monsters now," Toby said. "I am sure this will end well."

"Relax, Toby. It's cute and small."

"The mom was probably once cute and small, too. Then she got big, grew fangs and claws, and started eating people for dinner," Toby said drily.

Scott wasn't really listening anymore, though. He was scratching the dragon's chin again as it gulped down its third hot dog.

"I think we'll call you Gorbash," Scott said, recalling a dragon from an old book he'd read.

"If I could barf, I would," Toby said.

TWENTY-EIGHT

C onvincing a baby dragon to go to sleep turned out to be much more work than getting it to eat. It took Scott a couple of hours to finally get Gorbash settled down.

The effort was complicated by the fact that he didn't want the dragon sleeping in the same compartment as the medical pod. When Hector woke up, he'd be disoriented for a bit and maybe still hurting. The last thing Scott wanted was for him to see a dragon waddling around first thing.

He had a feeling the chief wouldn't approve of his choice in pets.

Gorbash was therefore bedded down in the crew compartment just aft of the medical and galley area. The place was a mess. Everything Scott owned had been tossed about by the rough landing. But he pulled a crate down from the storage hold, emptied the food packets out of it, and placed the dragon inside.

It complained for a bit, but Scott stuck several more hot dogs into the crate. The hatchling wolfed them all down and eventually grew tired enough to curl up and fall asleep. Scott sealed the crate up. It had plenty of holes for air, but it would keep the dragon from getting into mischief unsupervised.

The sun was already rising, and Scott hadn't gotten nearly enough sleep. There were still a good many hours before Tamara was due to come back and pick up her father.

"I'm going to catch a quick nap," Scott said. "Watch the monitors, and keep an eye on Gorbash for me?"

"A good thing one of us is able to stay awake," Toby replied.

Yeah, he had to agree with that. Having Toby along had made the trip much less lonesome, but the dog was proving to be a lifesaver now that he was back on Earth again.

"I'm glad Mom sent you along with me," Scott said, rolling over to face the robot.

But Toby was already off to the cockpit, where he'd keep an eye out for trouble. Scott could always feel secure with Toby at his back. He smiled, rolled back over, and went to sleep.

SCOTT'S TABLET buzzed him awake an hour before noon. He checked on Gorbash, who was still sleeping. Then he looked in on Hector. The pod continued to work on him, but his legs already looked much better.

A few taps on the diagnostic panel showed him what the pod had managed to do. New bone had been printed and inserted into the shattered areas, then bonded in place with surgical glue. Tears to several major blood vessels were repaired. The incisions had then been sealed back up with more glue. All told, the injury was still bad. The pod had wrapped up each lower leg with a hard plastic cast, printed around each limb to hold the bones in place. Hector would be a long time healing, but he'd recover.

"Any problems while I was asleep?" Scott asked, peeking down into the cockpit.

"All quiet on the western front," Toby replied.

"Good. Maybe things will stay that way."

"Fat chance," Toby said.

"Pessimist."

"Realist," Toby replied. Scott chuckled and went back up into the galley.

Breathing easy about some things finally going right, Scott sat down to a quick brunch before Tamara returned. That brought up another potential problem. His food stores weren't that great. The Stargazer shipped out on a two year mission. He'd brought along extra food, just in case there was some sort of problem on the journey. But food weighed a lot, and there was a limit to how much mass the rocket could accelerate to a high enough velocity.

The short of it was he had less than three months of food left. Maybe a bit more than that if he rationed a bit. Feeding the dragon plus himself, it was probably going to be a lot less than three months.

"Not an insurmountable problem," he said aloud. The people living here had to be eating something, after all. He just hoped their diet wasn't mostly mushrooms. They lived in tunnels, so it was possible. Scott hated mushrooms.

"Company coming down the hill," Toby called out. "Oh, looks like there is a whole lot of company coming down the hill. Armed for bear. Or robot dog and weirdo pilot, as the case might be."

Scott stuffed the last of breakfast into his mouth and tossed the trash into his recycler. The ship had to have enough plastic to 3D print an entire army of little toys and gadgets after three years of recycling the stuff. Now that plastic was an irreplaceable commodity, Scott was glad he'd kept the stuff around.

He darted forward into the cockpit and slid down beside Toby. The cameras were aimed at a hillside a short distance away. It was the same hill he and Tamara rushed down to get to the ship. It wasn't empty anymore, though. Nor was it a small band of people coming to pick up their chief on a litter.

"Holy shit. How many of them are there?" Scott asked, trying to count.

"Eighty-eight," Toby replied. "It looks like two distinct groups of roughly equal size. See how the ones on the right have short swords instead of spears?"

"We're looking at two groups?" Scott asked. Tamara had implied there was more than one band of humans left alive, but he hadn't thought to ask much about the politics of the area. Were they all friends? If so, why bring such a massive group to his ship?

"I don't like the look of this at all," Toby said.

"But there's Tamara," Scott said, tapping the screen.

She was at the front of the spear-carrying group. Alongside her was a man wearing thick hides, a sword belted at his waist. Tamara was talking to him, but it looked like he was ignoring her. That didn't sit well with her. Scott could see the fiery look on her face as he zoomed in the lens.

"Definitely not a good friend of hers," he said. "And a hell of a lot more company than we were planning to receive."

"You should probably go wake up sleeping chiefy."

"Agreed," Scott said.

Maybe Hector could sort out whatever mess was

headed their way. He glanced back at the screen again, not liking the look of things there at all. That didn't look like a group gathered to bring their injured chief home.

It looked like a small army on the road to a battle, and they were headed his way.

TWENTY-NINE

Tamara kept a firm grip on her spear, working hard at maintaining just as strong a grip on her emotions. Losing control would only hurt her case, and their position was precarious enough as it was. Things were moving far faster than anyone would have guessed.

"There is the ship," she said.

The man walking next to her made a "Hmph" noise in his throat. He didn't seem impressed.

"It doesn't look like a ship to me. Seems more like another abandoned tower from the old times," he said.

"It's a ship from the sky," Tamara said.

His eyebrows shot up, and she wondered if she'd revealed one thing too many. But the only way to deal with people like Yaven was through power. If he thought you were weak, he would strike. Hero's Keep had only retained possession of their home because they were strong.

With her father out of commission, that was apparently in question.

Yaven had been waiting at Hero's Keep when she

arrived, a small army at his back. The guards had refused him entrance, thank god. He had been irate about that but had cooled down once she had met with him.

His spy network had to be even better than Hector had guessed for him to get word of her father's injury so swiftly. Yaven was all but ready to jump in and take over Hero's Keep.

Tamara's people would have none of it. Even if her father had fallen, it was assumed she would take over their lead. Once she had assured them he was alive and healing, their faith increased even more.

Yaven was left with little choice but to act the part of the concerned neighbor. He and his men camped outside the Keep, then traveled back to Scott's ship in the morning.

"You say this stranger killed a dragon?" Yaven asked.

"Two, that I know of. One was slain before I met him. The other he killed in front of my eyes," Tamara said.

"We don't have any records of our people ever killing a dragon," Yaven admitted.

"Neither do we."

"Yet this stranger killed two in the space of a few days. He must be an amazing warrior," Yaven replied.

They were nearing the base of the ship. Soon Yaven would get to see for himself. Tamara kept a firm grip on her weapon. The neighboring chief hadn't brought a war band because he was going on a quiet romp. There might well be fighting before the day was over. Her people were ready for it, if necessary.

Tamara stopped at the base of the ship and looked up.

"Do we need to knock?" Yaven asked. The mocking notes in his voice were irritating as hell.

"No. Scott saw us coming some time ago," she replied.

Before Yaven could make another sarcastic remark, the

hatch halfway up the ship opened. Her father sat there, waving down to them.

He looked well. Better than she'd been expecting, to be honest. His cheeks had lost their pallor. His face showed no signs of pain.

Hector shifted so that his legs hung out, and Tamara caught a glimpse of bright color beneath his pants. She wasn't sure what that could be. Some part of the treatment Scott's pod had used to help heal him?

"I see you brought company," Hector called down.

"Yes, they insisted on coming along," she replied.

"To make certain you were well, Hector," Yaven said. He sketched a half-assed bow.

Like hell. His motivation was simpler than that. Yaven had always wanted their Keep for his own people. He'd tried taking it twice in Tamara's memory. Both times, his people had failed to get past even the outer wall. They'd been forced to retreat. The Keep was well defended, the walls hard to breach.

But like any fox, Yaven was always watching for signs of weakness. Tamara's father knew the man's game and was trying to display strength. She wondered just how healed he really was.

"Come down, my friend. We will share food and drink, and talk of your battle with the dragon. I am interested to hear about it," Yaven said.

Hector turned and said something to a person who was out of sight. That would be Scott, she figured. Or maybe his dog. The idea of a talking dog took a little getting used to, but it was growing on her.

Then her father looped rope around his waist and tied it off. He slipped over the edge, cautious of his legs. She could see the wince on his face every time one of his shins banged into anything.

Slowly the rope lowered Hector back to the ground. Once he was there, he sat on the soft soil, breathing hard. Even the short downward journey had exhausted him. Tamara looked over at Yaven to see what he made of the display.

His face looked thoughtful and distracted. Would he see that as weakness, and use her father's injury as an excuse to attack?

Then Hector stood. He rose slowly, using the ship to keep his balance. But he was at last standing. Tamara's heart leapt with joy. She hadn't been sure her father would ever be able to stand again. The injuries to his legs had been so severe. But there he was, weak but on his feet.

"I am told I should be resting my legs as often as possible to spare them damage. If you will come to me, Yaven?" Hector asked.

"Of course, my friend," Yaven replied. He strode over to Hector. Tamara tightened her grip on the spear. If they were going to strike, it would happen soon.

But Yaven didn't attack her father. Instead, he helped Hector take a seat on the ground and then sat down across from him. Yaven clapped his hands together, and two of his men rushed forward bearing fruit and a flask of water. He held the flask out to Hector, who drank and then returned it. Yaven drank from the flask next.

"Momentous times we live in," Yaven said. "Men can kill dragons now, I hear."

"You hear about things far more quickly than I would credit to rumors alone," Hector said.

"I have my ways of gathering information. I am good to people. They return in kind. For example, I knew of your injury," Yaven said. "But my information said you were much more gravely hurt than you seem now."

"I heal quickly," Hector said.

"And these?" Yaven asked, tapping fingers on the colored wraps around Hector's lower legs. The raps made a hollow sound. The stuff looked like cloth, but it was hard to the touch. Remarkable material.

"A gift from our new friend and ally," Hector said. Then he called in a loud voice up to the ship. "Scott, could you join us?"

Scott popped his head out the airlock door. "I would be glad to."

A short climb down the ladder and Scott too was on the ground. Tamara noticed that he'd changed his clothing, but he was still wearing the gun on his hip.

Good. He knew enough to be armed at a meeting like this. Scott didn't look especially impressive, but the gun might stave off a real battle. At least for the time being.

"You are the man who killed a dragon?" Yaven asked. He didn't even try to keep the incredulity from his voice as he looked Scott up and down.

In response, Scott drew his pistol. Before Yaven could utter another word, Scott fired the gun into the ground a short distance from Yaven's feet. Clods of earth flew into the air, showering Yaven's legs with dirt.

"Two, actually. Yes, I am the dragonslayer you're looking for. Now, who are you, and why are you here at my ship?"

THIRTY

To Scott's surprise, Yaven didn't flinch away from the gunshot. Most of his men did, but their leader simply stood there, eyes meeting Scott's. Either he was made of incredibly stern stuff, or...

"I have seen such a weapon before," Yaven said, gesturing to the pistol Scott still held. "When I was a child. It was a relic pulled from the old ruins. My father showed me how it worked. Much like a bow, but the power inside sent a projectile much further than an arrow."

That was interesting. If these people still had access to fragments of tech, it gave Scott hope that there might be more of it out there, waiting to be found. Even if most of the guns and ammunition were spent or ruined by time, there might be other fragments of his old world still surviving.

"Where did you find it?" Scott asked.

"It was long ago. I know not where. The weapon broke when someone fired it while I was still young. Almost blew his hand off," Yaven said with a chuckle at the memory. "Believe me, if I knew where I could get more such weapons, I would definitely have already done so."

The threat in his words was only thinly veiled. Scott holstered the pistol, since it was obviously stirring up Yaven's greed. Shit, the whole of the Stargazer would be a treasure trove for anyone who won it. Assuming they could figure out how to operate any of the devices inside, anyway.

"Too bad. It would have been nice to find more such things," Scott said.

"Indeed," Yaven replied.

"Enough of this. Why are you here?" Hector asked.

"Chief of Hero's Keep, I heard you were hurt. I led a party of my best warriors to see for myself," Yaven said.

"He was waiting at the Keep when I got back," Tamara said.

"Was he? And how did you hear about my injury so quickly, Yaven?" Hector asked.

"I have many means of finding out information that is of interest to me," Yaven said.

"Many spies," Tamara spat out.

It was clear there was no love lost between these people. Yaven's attitude turned Scott off from the first words he uttered. If he was going to come down on one side or the other in this argument, he knew which way his alliance was going to fall. For all that Hector had locked him in a cell, the man had been decent since.

"You have seen. I am alive and healing. Are you satisfied?" Hector asked.

"I have seen. But I am disturbed by what I see. You ally yourself with this man, Hector, and threaten the balance of power of the entire land. How many of these gun weapons does he have?" Yaven asked. "Just the one? Or are there a hundred more in his tower there?"

Scott opened his mouth to tell Yaven his arsenal wasn't anywhere near that large, and that it was for his use alone.

But Tamara caught his eyes with a glance and gave him a small shake of the head. He closed his mouth again without saying anything.

"Afraid, Yaven?" Hector said, smiling as he came back to his feet. It was clear it hurt the man to stand, but he wasn't letting that stop him. Hector had picked up a stick and was using it to support his weight. He took two steady steps toward Yaven. "You should be."

There was a flicker of fear across Yaven's face before he replaced the look with a mask of furious anger. Oh, he was scared of Hector all right. Frightened enough to be dangerous, even. If Scott could see that, he figured everyone else watching could as well.

"Afraid? Of you and a few toys?" Yaven laughed. "We shall soon see who has more to fear."

Then he whirled and stalked away. His men fell in beside him, marching up the hill and away from the Stargazer.

"How much trouble are we facing from him?" Scott asked.

"Not much," Hector said, easing himself back to the ground. "Those were most of his fighters he brought. We can raise twice that number. He would be a fool to attack us. All the same, have your warriors spread out to stay alert nearby, Tamara."

"Yes, father." She stepped away from them, barking orders to the men and women who'd come with her from the Keep.

Scott didn't like what the man had said about the balance of power. He wasn't trying to be a power-broker or anything of the sort. But he didn't understand the politics binding these groups of humans together, and it felt like he was in over his head.

"You shouldn't be standing yet," Scott told Hector to change the subject.

"My legs are telling me that, thank you," Hector replied, grimacing.

"But you were walking, father! It's amazing, just like I told you," Tamara said as she came back over. All her warriors had moved out in pairs, scouting the area around the ship.

"It is indeed. I look at such technology and wonder how many lives it might have saved over the past year. Which in turn makes me think what other secrets might be hidden inside your ship, Scott," Hector said.

Scott's eyes narrowed. He'd had just about enough of people trying to take things away from him when they felt like it. "My secrets are well protected."

"No fear, my friend. There is blood and battle between us. You have saved my daughter's life and healed me," Hector said. "You have my friendship for life. But there are many tribes of men living in these lands. Word of your ship and its wonders will spread. Eventually, others will come and try to take these things from you."

"Well, shit," Scott said.

He could fight to defend the ship, but he wasn't going to get her flight-worthy again while fending off an endless series of attacks. He ran a hand through his hair, trying to figure out what might work. He needed breathing room more than anything else. Time and space to figure out how to get the ship running again so he could cross the continent. Was the cure even there? He had to hope so. If he lost even that glimmer of hope, then he didn't know what he would do.

"As much as it pains me to say this, I think it would be best for my people, as well as for you, if you left this place as swiftly as possible," Hector said softly. "I would offer you what hospitality I can for as long as you wish to stay. You've earned that. But the longer you are here, the more danger will come calling."

"I think you're right. Leaving sounds like the best plan," Scott said. He was surprised to feel a pang of remorse as he said the words. Was he already growing attached to these people? He smiled ruefully. "Unfortunately, my ship is upside-down, and I don't have anything close to the tools to get her righted."

"I think we can help with that," Hector said. "It will be a mighty feat of engineering, but my people are excellent with pulley, level, block, and tackle. We lifted the stones that make up our walls using such methods."

Scott's eyebrows shot up. Those rocks were huge. The Stargazer was many times larger, but for the first time in a while, he had hope they might be able to accomplish something.

"It's worth a try," Scott said.

"I will send for my people. We begin work today," Hector said. He glanced north, in the direction Yaven and his warriors had departed. "I have the sense that time is of the essence."

THIRTY-ONE

"**W**hen Hector said he was sending for his people, he wasn't kidding around," Toby observed from the cockpit.

"He doesn't do things in half measures, that's for sure," Scott replied.

He'd offered to let Tamara and Hector stay with him in the ship after their conversation. Scott wanted to show them that he trusted them. Hector seemed to understand his intent but had declined with a smile, saying he and his daughter would remain with their people. They camped at the base of the ship.

By the time Scott woke for the day, people from the Keep were already flooding into the area. It looked like every able-bodied person living in the tunnels was down there. Hundreds of people, young and old, ran around carrying out various tasks. Small children were setting up water stations. Women and men were unloading carts full of rope and equipment. If the force the day before had looked like an army, this seemed more like a barn-raising on a massive scale.

"I think I'd better go downstairs and welcome them," Scott said.

"Fed your dragon yet today?" Toby asked.

"No! Shoot. I'd better go see to Gorbash." Scott cursed under his breath. He wasn't used to having pets. Toby was great, because he didn't need feeding. The dragon hatchling had to be hungry as hell by now. He'd fed it before going to bed, and it had curled up in its little bin again. But Gorbash was still asleep when he got up.

Toby followed Scott as he snatched another packet of hot dogs and climbed up to his cabin. He turned around and gave the dog a look.

"Shouldn't you be keeping an eye on our guests?" Scott asked.

"Oh, I think this is much more interesting."

"Seriously, Toby. You've had it in for Gorbash from minute one. He's cute and little. What's your problem with him?" Scott asked.

"He's a dragon. He might be cute right now, but what's he going to look like when he's full grown?" Toby asked.

"It's not an issue. Gorbash is totally under control," Scott said. He shoved open the hatch to his quarters.

Which looked like a tornado had swept through it.

His clothes were everywhere. Half of them were shredded. Stuffing from the bed drifted around on gentle gusts of air from the ventilation system. The place was completely trashed.

Gorbash stuck his nose out from the hole he'd tunneled into the mattress.

"Mrrp?"

"Completely under control? Whatever you say, Khaleesi," Toby said. Then he turned around and clomped down the wall back to the cockpit, chuckling all the way.

"Gorbash, get down here right now," Scott said.

"Mrrp!"

"Right this instant," he repeated, pointing at the deck in front of him.

"Mrrp," Gorbash said. Then he jumped from the mattress.

At first, Scott thought the dragon was going to fall and moved to catch him. But the thin lines of ribbing along Gorbash's wings glowed when he was midway to the floor, and he stopped falling. He fluttered his wings, gently moving around. The hatchling skimmed past Scott, fanning him with his wings. He had to laugh. The little critter was clearly pleased with himself and his newfound ability.

"That's right, you are a good little dragon," Scott said. "Now how are you managing to do that?"

He watched the wings. When Gorbash wanted to go up, they grew brighter, and when he descended, they became dim. The glow was clearly related to dragonflight. He'd seen that before. But what was the underlying mechanism?

"Come here, fella," Scott said, holding out a hot dog.

"Mrrp!"

Gorbash flew over and snapped it from his fingers, gulping the food down. Scott descended back down the ladder from his room, holding out another hot dog. The dragon followed and chomped that one down too.

"Good boy. Keep coming, now," Scott said. He fed the dragon another chunk of meat, slowly leading it across the room.

Then he laid the entire rest of the package down inside the medical pod. Gorbash happily descended upon the food and wolfed down the hot dogs. While it was distracted by the food, Scott tapped the controls on the pod, which lowered the lid on his pet dragon.

"Mrrp?" Gorbash said, looking up as the lid sealed shut.

"Relax, little buddy. Just a quick medical exam to see what you're all about," Scott said. There was a hiss as the pod sealed and vented in a gas to ease the dragon into sleep.

He crossed his fingers, hoping the sleeping chemical would work on Gorbash. This was an entirely different biology. Adult dragons could fly in space. Did they even need to breathe? It might not work at all.

But the dragon sniffed the air, gave a few chirps, and sneezed. Then he curled up around itself in a small circle, laid his head down on his tail, and fell asleep.

"I don't know whether that was the gas or the food. Either way, he's asleep now," Scott said.

He set the pod to do a full diagnostic on Gorbash. The more he knew about how these animals worked, the better off he was going to be. Sure, he'd beaten two of them so far, but the first was by luck, and the second was a near thing. He needed intel on this enemy.

It was hard to think about little Gorbash as an enemy, but even if he was cute and friendly, the bigger ones certainly were not. They were probably responsible for the downfall of human civilization. If Scott was going to have a chance of bringing any of it back, he needed to do something about the dragons.

Bringing it back. Wow, that was the first time he'd had that thought. Scott shook his head. He was no leader. All he wanted was to find the cure that would extend his life. Someone else could do the heavy lifting of bringing back strip malls and chain department stores.

"Time to go see our friends," Scott said. He went to the airlock.

THIRTY-TWO

By the time Scott had climbed down to join the people from the Keep, the work was already in full swing. People climbed trees all around the Stargazer, looping long ropes over thick boughs, then running them through a series of complex pulley systems. He'd never seen such intricate ropework.

"This puts the Boy Scouts to shame," he told Hector. The chief was seated in the middle of everything, directing traffic and solving problems as they came up.

"These Scouts are good with rope?" Hector asked.

"They're some of the best where I come from," Scott replied.

Hector canted his head at an angle. "And where precisely are you from, Scott Free? You haven't said."

Scott turned away and stared at the sky. Where he was from wasn't the question. He'd been born a few hundred miles from this very spot. Hell, he'd driven through the Hero Tunnel more than once. This was his world. This was his home.

And yet it was entirely alien at the same time. How did

you explain time travel to someone from a place and time like this? Sure, he hadn't literally traveled in time, but it was close enough to count. He couldn't imagine Hector understanding.

"You wouldn't believe me if I told you," Scott said, the words bitter ashes. No one from this time would believe him or ever understand him. He was alone.

"Try me, my friend," Hector said softly.

Something about his voice made Scott turn back to him. He looked into the other man's eyes. They were stern, yes. But Scott saw kindness and compassion there as well.

"I can see you are hurting. Is it because you want to go back to this place you think I won't believe?" Hector asked.

"No. I can't ever go home. It's dead and gone," Scott said.

"Destroyed? Even with your weapons and powers?"

"Hector, you said to try you. I'll be clear. I'm from here. I was born not too far from this place. I remember this world when the roads were full of cars, the skies full of airplanes, and everyone had a pocket computer," Scott said. "I'm from here. Here, but four hundred years ago."

"Ah, I had a feeling it might be something like that," Hector said.

"You did?" Scott asked, astonished.

"Yes. You couldn't be from this world. Technology like yours? We would have heard about it before now, would be not?" Hector asked.

"Yes, probably," Scott said.

Which was part of his worry. After all, if any tech sufficient to cure him existed on Earth, the people with that power would surely have been out fighting dragons and trying to restore the world. That nobody was actively out there in fighter planes shooting down dragons meant there probably wasn't anyone capable of doing so.

It made the odds of finding a cure for his condition slim.

"In the past you came from, this was before the dragons came?" Hector asked.

"Yeah. Dragons were just a bedtime story for us," Scott said.

"Why leave all that and come here, then?" Hector asked. "You left behind your family, friends, everyone you knew? For what?"

Scott laughed bitterly. "Because I needed something I thought I could only get in the future."

Somehow, coming clean about everything felt right. Hector was helping him without knowing about his disease. Scott didn't have to worry the man would assist him out of pity. He'd earned the chief's trust and admiration. Time to return it with a little trust of his own. He tapped his skull.

"I have a disease. Inherited from my father," Scott said. "I don't know when it will start affecting me, but when it does, I will gradually lose the ability to sleep. Then my brain will degenerate. I'll go mad. See things. Eventually die as a drooling idiot."

Hector was silent for a long moment. "You watched your own father die this way?" he asked softly.

"Yes."

"That is a hard thing to bear," Hector said, reaching out a hand to touch Scott's shoulder. "My own father died in battle with Yaven's clan. Quick and clean. A good death. I can see why you would fear the fate which befell your father. How can I help?"

Scott thought about the question a moment. At first he wanted to shout at Hector, to tell the man there was nothing he could do to help. That the cure he'd sacrificed everything to find was likely lost along with the rest of human civilization. But Hector wasn't asking to be hurtful. He honestly wanted to give whatever aid he could.

"You already are helping," Scott said. "The last word I had was that a cure for my condition was available in California. On the far coast from here. About three thousand miles away."

"A long walk," Hector said. "But with your ship?"

"A few hours flight time."

"It goes so fast?" Hector asked. Scott nodded. "Perhaps you'll take me up in it sometime."

"If we get it flying again, I absolutely will," Scott said.

He felt his mood lifting. It had been too big a secret to keep to himself. Sharing felt right. Hector might only understand part of what he'd said, but the man understood the human part of Scott's problems, and... that was enough.

Work continued through the morning. By noon, a team was hauling the dragon carcass down from the top of the ship. Scott noticed another crew digging at the earth under the ship, cutting the dragon out from beneath it.

"Why worry about the bodies?" Scott asked Tamara.

"Dragon carcasses attract dragons. We don't know why, but they're pretty consistent about it," she replied. "We're lucky that body up there hasn't already brought more."

"What do you plan to do with the bodies?" Scott asked. He eyed the wings thoughtfully as her people lowered the body down using the rope and pulley system.

"Use most of it. The meat isn't edible, but we don't waste anything we can use. Teeth, horns, claws, scales, all of it has value for us," Tamara said.

"Can I take the wings?" Scott asked. He still didn't know what the material inside them was, but he was curious to know more. It had to be related to the dragons' flight in some way.

She looked at him oddly but nodded. Scott ended up with the ribs from all four wings stowed away aboard the ship by the time he was done. He'd also ruined another set of clothing chopping the ribs out of the wings.

This reminded him that most of his clothes were shredded. He tossed the messed up ones — along with all the clothes Gorbash had ruined — into the recycler, and he programmed the printer to make him a few new sets of clothes. He was down to his last clean outfit when he checked on Gorbash, who was still sleeping it off in the pod. The medical computer was still collating data about the dragon, but it had already run a ton of scans. Scott started looking over the information. Damned if the dragons weren't pretty similar to life forms from Earth. Was it a quirk of evolution, or something else entirely?

Screams from outside startled him from his work. He dashed to the airlock and opened it, peering out. At first Scott wasn't sure what was going on. People dashed every which way. Then he caught the whiff of smoke and turned to face the north.

Smoke was rising from the trees in that direction. The forest was on fire.

THIRTY-THREE

Scott slid down the ladder and hit the ground running. Tamara had already rejoined her father at his command post. He was shouting orders, and Scott didn't think it wise to disturb him. Hector knew better than he did how to combat the threat they were facing.

"He's sent half our guard force north to see how bad the fire is," Tamara said.

"What can we do if it's bad?" Scott asked.

"From here? Not much. The nearest river is a mile away. We have enough drinking water but nowhere near enough to put out a fire. Will your ship survive if the flames reach it?" she asked.

"I wish I knew," Scott said.

The Stargazer was a tough piece of engineering. She was designed to handle massive stress, as evidenced by the way she'd weathered the crash landing. Would the ship be flightworthy after the trees heated up the air around it? He had a feeling that even if the ship's structure survived, most of the systems and components would be shot.

Smoke filled the air as the breeze carried it through the

camp around his ship. It was thick, but he didn't feel a lot of heat in the air. Maybe the fire was still a ways out and they had time to divert it?

He reached up and activated his radio.

"Toby, you seeing this?" Scott asked.

"The fog rolling in? Sure. Hard to miss."

"It's not fog, Toby."

"I know that. It's... never mind. What can I do for you?" Toby asked. Scott heard the dog sigh.

"Can you get me eyes on those flames?" Scott asked.

"A drone? Can do," Toby said.

"Make it so," Scott said with a grin. Then he turned to Tamara. "Now you get to see something cool."

A moment later, something shot away from the side of the ship, making a buzzing noise as it flew by. Scott pulled out his pocket tablet and called up the drone's camera feed. It zipped between the trees, streaking past the scout party Hector sent north. Moments later it was closing on the flames.

"That's amazing!" Tamara said.

"Are fires like this common around here?" Scott asked. It seemed strange to him. The whole place was incredibly boggy. Everything ought to be too wet to burn easily.

"Rare, but they have happened," she said.

"What do you do about them?"

"We gather inside the Keep and stay there until the fires go out."

Scott had to remind himself that these people didn't have twenty-first century firefighting technology. The best they could do would be chop down trees and throw buckets of water on a flame. It would be like peeing on a campfire.

The drone came up on the flames, but they were nowhere near as large as Scott expected. The trees themselves weren't ablaze at all. Instead, it looked like a brush fire on the ground, more of a smoldering mess of branches than a real forest fire. The wet branches were producing far more smoke than the small fire around them would normally have done.

"It's a tiny fire," Scott said. "We're OK."

Then he had the drone zoom in closer to the piles of branches. The piles were in a straight line. That didn't look anything like a natural occurence. He tapped a key to zoom in on a branch.

The end was clean cut.

"We've got trouble," Scott said, already putting away the tablet and running for the ship. "Warn your father. The smoke isn't a real fire. It's a ruse to draw people away from the camp."

"What? Why?" she asked.

"Why would you want to draw defenders away from a place?" Scott asked. "To make an attack easier."

He saw understanding in her eyes a she turned and darted toward her father. Scott climbed the ladder back up to the ship, considering what he had for defenses available. It wasn't much. When all this was over, he was going to have the printer make him some damned armor. It would have been nice if the Stargazer had side-mounted turrets, too.

"Might as well ask for a platoon of Marines," he muttered. That would be even nicer than the turrets, to be honest.

"Boss. What do you want me to do?" Toby asked, meeting him just inside the airlock.

He looked over the dog. Toby wasn't built for fighting, but he was made of metal. The robot could take a pounding and come through OK. Scott hated the idea of even risking the loss of his oldest friend, but this was all-or-nothing time. If the enemy force he knew had to be coming won this fight, the ship and everything on it would be lost.

"We're going to have to fight them off," Scott said. "You up for that?"

"Activating combat protocols," Toby said in a voice that sounded remarkably like Scott's mother.

"Combat protocols? What combat protocols?" Scott asked. She'd never told him the robot had combat protocols. He watched as Toby stepped through the airlock and begin walking down the side of the ship.

"Damn. Going to need to have a chat with my dog," Scott said.

He opened the weapons locker and examined what he had left in there. The massive fifty caliber rifle was probably overkill for this. Besides, he only had so many bullets for that gun, and he wanted to save them for dealing with dragons.

That left the .44 pistol Scott was already carrying everywhere he went, an AR-15 rifle, and a magazine-fed shotgun. He eyeballed the latter two. Much as he thought the shotgun had more 'shock and awe' value, there was also a good chance he'd nail friends in the melee along with enemies.

"The AR it is, then," he said. He grabbed the weapon and loaded a combat vest with magazines, feeling wildly out of place the whole time.

This wasn't a movie. This was the real world. He wasn't some damned action hero. Once spears and whatever else started flying, any of them could take him out as easily as the snap of a finger.

Something else was bothering Scott, much as he was trying to put it from his mind. He'd never killed a person.

He'd slain the dragon to save Tamara, but people were different. Could he do it? He eyed the rifle cradled in his arms. Could he pull the trigger and take a human life?

Damn these people for fighting each other when there were so many better things the remnants of humanity could be doing. But then, humans had always been stupid that way. Was there ever a time when people weren't fighting each other?

Scott slung the rifle across his back and ran to the airlock, sealing the inner door behind him. He'd be back soon enough — he hoped.

THIRTY-FOUR

H ector stood in the middle of a swarming ball of frenzied activity as Scott approached. Tamara had clearly reached him with a warning. He was surrounded with a small troop of armed warriors, all watchful. Three of them were eyeing Toby, spears aimed in his direction.

It was apparent why as soon as Scott looked at the dog. Toby generally walked around looking something like a metal golden retriever. Every step oozed a sense of trustworthiness and good virtue. He'd been designed to inspire those feelings.

This Toby was something very different. He looked like he always had, but at the same time different. Every movement had a sharp, predatory look to it. None of his physical features were any different, but it was like having an angry wolf in your midst instead of a fluffy lapdog.

"Toby, cool it down a bit before one of these guys spears you," Scott said. Then he turned to the warriors. "He's a friend, guys. Plus, your spears won't do anything more than annoy him."

He wasn't sure if that made the spearmen feel better or worse. They lowered the spears, but they were still eyeing Toby like he might rip their throats out at any moment. The robot didn't even have teeth! Scott wondered if the dog's "combat protocols" could do anything more than growl and look mean.

Knowing his mother, they probably could.

He stalked through the wall of guards and reached Hector. Tamara was nowhere in sight, but her father was busily donning armor. A spear rested against a log beside him.

"What do you think you're doing?" Scott asked. "Those leg bones have barely started healing. You over-stress them, they're going to snap like twigs."

"You think a chief can sit idly by while his people fight?" Hector asked. "Tamara gave me your warning, then took scouts south. She thinks the attack will come from that direction, opposite the smoke."

It was possible. They could try to come in from the opposite side. There was an easy way to find out, of course.

"Toby, run a sweep with the drone. Find our bad guys," Scott said.

"On it," Toby replied. His usual banter was gone.

Two more drones shot from the ship, joining the first in their hunt. That was his entire compliment of the little quad-copters. He'd worried bringing them would be useless, but they were proving well worth the pounds of weight they'd cost. Another little bit of survival gear his mother had foisted off on him.

She'd hoped Scott would find the peaceful, advanced world he was looking for. But she pointed out to him that humanity had as many stumbles as it did rises. It was possible he'd come back in the middle of a war, a plague, a famine, or who knew what else. She'd made sure he prepared for almost any eventuality. The Stargazer's storage hold was full of boxes she'd sent along, some of which Scott hadn't even opened yet.

"Got them. Two forces. One coming in from the west, and a larger one from the south," Toby said.

"How many men?" Hector asked.

"Twenty to the west. One hundred and twelve from the south," Toby replied.

"Damn. That many?" Hector said. He ran fingers through his beard. "That can't be just Yaven. He's found allies to help him."

"What do we have to work with?" Scott asked.

"I send thirty men north to the fire. I sent a boy running after them as soon as Tamara warned me of the ruse, but they won't be back for a while," Hector said. "Tamara has another forty armed people with her, and I have forty more here, although most of them are not warriors."

"What about the rest of these people?" Scott asked. The camp housed at least a couple hundred men, women, and children.

"Not trained," Hector said. He coughed from the smoke. "They can swing a stick, but they'll fall like nothing before trained warriors."

"Got it. Reinforce Tamara, then. I'll take the west side," Scott said.

"By yourself?" Hector asked.

"I won't be alone. I'll have Toby," Scott replied.

"Good luck, then."

"You too."

Scott started off toward the west side of the ship, hoping he could cash the check he'd just written. There were twenty trained fighters coming at him. Those kinds of numbers were crazy to think about, but he had all the advantages he could ask for.

"Don't miss," Toby said.

"Thanks. Be careful out there. You're annoying as hell, but you're still the best friend I've got," Scott said.

"Aw, all mushy right before the fight," Toby replied. "I've got eyes on the enemy. Two drones are monitoring our combat zone. They're coming forward at a slow jog. Not even trying to use cover."

Why would they? Yaven saw him fire a pistol one time, sure. But they'd never seen the carnage a semi-automatic assault rifle could create. Scott found a position behind a fallen tree trunk directly in the enemy's path. He pulled a second magazine from his vest and laid it next to him on the trunk. They he aimed the rifle ahead and waited.

It felt like forever before he saw the first human stepping around a tree into the clear space ahead of him. It couldn't have been more than a minute or so, though.

"Target in the kill zone," Toby said. "Recommend waiting until you have three targets before engaging."

Sure, just think of them as targets. Little pop-ups, like on the range. Not human beings who were going to bleed once his bullets hit them. Scott swallowed hard.

A second man stepped out behind the first, then gestured behind him. One after another, more people flowed around the tree. Three, then four, then five, and more kept coming. Scott's breath came in rapid gasps.

"What are you doing? Engage targets!" Toby's voice said in his ear.

Scott couldn't move. His finger was on the trigger. One of the warriors was lined up in his sights. But he couldn't fire. Sweat poured down his face, stinging his eyes.

"Oh, for the love of... one dog, coming to the rescue," Toby said.

Then the robot all but exploded out of the brush near the enemy warriors. He hit one of them hard, tackling him to the ground. The man went down without even a chance to call out.

The others around him saw the attack, though. They all had swords in their hands. Together they turned and raised their blades, preparing to cut the robot to bits.

"No!" Scott shouted. His finger jerked on the trigger.

One warrior went down. Scott moved the rifle a centimeter to the right and fired again. Another man went down. Over and over he kept it up, aiming and firing. The warriors didn't even seem to know what was happening. Some of them crouched down in the ferns, but those were no cover against bullets.

Finally, they'd had enough. The remaining men called out to each other, backing up around the tree in full retreat. Two of them pulled back wounded men, dragging them to safety. Scott let those go. He already felt sick enough to his stomach with what he'd done.

"You did it," Toby said. "Good shooting."

Scott stood up and walked toward the carnage he'd wrought.

"I wouldn't," Toby warned.

He kept going. Scott needed to see what he'd done with his own eyes.

When he did, his stomach finally rebelled, and he threw up.

THIRTY-FIVE

The clearing around the Stargazer was in chaos as Scott returned. He'd let the remaining warriors go, hoping they would keep on retreating. Toby had a drone following them to make sure they did, but the drone watching the southern fight was showing a battle that wasn't going well for Hector's people.

Scott shouldered the rifle and drew his pistol. He'd grabbed a sword from one of the men he'd killed. It was more like machete than a real sword, but it felt good in his hand.

He strode past his ship to where the battle was being waged in a straight line. Hector stood in the middle, fighting an even bigger man wielding a massive axe.

"Toby, help Hector," he said.

"What about you?"

"I'll be fine," Scott lied.

Nothing was going to be fine again. He'd killed people. He was a killer, and it didn't feel good at all. That those warriors he'd shot planned to do the same thing to him and Tamara and all her people didn't make a lot of difference.

But Scott had discovered something during the brief fight. He might not enjoy killing people, but he was pretty damned good at it, at least in this world where he was the only person with a gun.

He walked up to the battle line, raising his pistol in one hand while still holding the sword in the other. He fired, and the man he'd been aiming at whipped around from the force of the impact. Scott wasn't sure where he'd hit, but with the .44, it barely mattered. Any impact was going to put someone down, at least for a while. Shooting from ten or fifteen feet away, it was almost impossible for him to miss.

The pistol's bolt locked to the rear sooner than he'd thought possible. Had he really spent an entire magazine already? Scott sheathed his sword, ejected the spent magazine, and inserted a new one. Taking the pistol in a two-handed grip this time, he continued to blast a massive hole in the enemy line.

Hector's warriors poured through the breach he made, cutting down enemies with their spears. The bolt locked back a second time. Numb to it all, Scott holstered the pistol. He was out of reloads for it, but the AR still had plenty of ammo left. He unslung the weapon from his shoulder.

Horns sounded, and the enemy force drew back, slowly at first and then retreating with even more speed. Scott aimed the rifle at their running figures. He could kill a few more as they fled, if he wanted to.

But he didn't want to. He wished more than anything that he'd never had to shoot anyone at all. There was no blood on his hands, but it felt like they might never be clean again.

Scott sank to his knees in the middle of the ruined men he'd killed and maimed, sobbing.

. . .

THEY FOUND HIM THAT WAY, as the battle ended and Hector's people counted their wounded and dead. Scott was vaguely aware of Toby growling at someone and looked up to see who it was.

"Scott, are you all right? Are you hurt?" It was Tamara.

"I'm not wounded," Scott said. His voice felt faint to his ears. "I'm not sure I am OK, though."

"Can I come through?" Tamara asked. Toby woofed, and she stepped closer and knelt beside Scott. "First battle?"

"Yes."

"It doesn't get any better, not for most of us," she said.

"How do you stand it?" Scott asked, looking up at her at last.

"Some people manage the pain of killing others by numbing themselves to it. They become cruel, cold, ruthless murderers. Others do their best to retain their humanity, in spite of the pain," she said. "You saved a lot of lives today, Scott."

He got slowly to his feet on rubber legs. But he looked around the battlefield. Warriors were helping each other, true. But there were also children there, running about and carrying water. Hector had brought more than fighters to help right his ship. All those noncombatants had been at risk as well. Scott looked at the kids running about, still alive because they'd fended off the attack.

"Yeah, there are worse things," he told Tamara. Then he looked around. "Where's Hector?"

She grimaced. "Hurt. Badly. Toby saved his life, but he was wounded, and at least one leg bone is broken again."

"Take me to him?"

"Of course," she said.

They went to an unwalled tent. In the middle lay Hector, a gash across his belly. His face was ashen, but his eyes lit up when he saw Scott.

"You survived. Thank you for your service to my people," Hector said.

Scott knelt beside him. "I will always do what I can to help a friend."

He looked over the wounds. Most of them were fairly superficial, but the belly wound looked serious. Scott couldn't see the full extent of the injury through the bandages over it, but it didn't look or smell good. Belly wounds could go septic in a heartbeat.

"You might need that pod again," Scott said.

Hector shook his head. "No. My people need me home. There were three clans besides Yaven's in that assault. He has rallied a mighty force to his side. They won't just strike here. They'll hit the Keep as well. We leave shortly."

"I have medicine that will help, then," Scott said. "Toby, get some antibiotics from the ship, please?"

The dog darted off. Hector flashed Scott a smile. "Always trying to show off your magic tricks, eh?"

"It's not magic; it's science," Scott said, returning the grin. "But yes. The medicine will help your body fight infection. Keep the wound from going bad."

Hector looked around and his face fell. "I am sorry."

"Sorry?" Scott asked.

"I told you I would help you get your ship in the air again. But I cannot. If we survive this war, then whatever is left of my people will give you what aid we can," Hector said.

"If you survive?"

"Hero's Keep is strong, but these are four clans allied against us. Our odds are not so good."

"I can..." Scott started to offer his help, but Hector cut him off with a slash of his hand.

"No, my friend. You have already done much. If you leave this place, the ship and all her treasure become vulnerable. Guard this hoard. If the enemy seizes it, we will be lost for certain."

Toby raced back over and deposited a small packet of medicine next to Hector. "Take two now, then one every half-day until they are all gone."

"I will do so, for as long as I have breath," Hector said.

Around them, the warband was rallying the rest of his people, gathering them into a close group to better protect them during the journey. The ropes and pulleys hung abandoned where they'd been placed in trees around the ship. They'd been so close to getting him aloft again, and now Scott felt like he was back to square one.

He couldn't blame them for leaving, though. They'd tried. Maybe when this mess was over, they could try again. In the meantime, Scott needed to retain control of the Stargazer.

Four men carefully lifted Hector's litter from the ground and joined the band. Scott waved. The chief and his daughter returned the gesture. Then the ranks of warriors stopped, and all faced toward him. They raised their spears high, and slammed them into the ground in unison.

"They honor you, Scott Free," Hector called out. "For your service. For your warrior spirit. For the lives of their loved ones you saved."

"Good luck, Chief Hector of Hero's Keep," Scott shouted back. "I expect to see you when this is all over."

"One way or another, I am sure you shall," Hector replied. Then his warband turned back toward the path for home.

Scott watched them all until they were out of sight before making the slow climb back up into his ship.

THIRTY-SIX

S cott stepped out of the airlock and into a disaster area. His first thought was Toby must have torn through supply lockers looking for the antibiotics, but that didn't make any sense. They were right in the medical cabinet.

Besides, many of the packets scattered all over the floor were opened. He reached down to scoop a few up. They were all food packets. Scott turned the open one over. It was a hot dog package.

"Mrrp?"

He looked back up and saw Gorbash hovering in mid-air in front of him. The dragon wasn't flapping his wings. He was just floating there, wings outstretched, with each of the bones running down through them glowing brightly.

"Now how the heck are you doing that?" Scott asked, the mess his dragon had made of the place forgotten for the moment.

He reached out toward Gorbash's wing. The dragon held still and let his hand move closer. Scott's fingers felt strange as they drew near, and the hairs on the back of his hand all stood up. On a hunch, he released the empty food packet he was holding a few inches away from the wing.

Like Gorbash, the packet simply hung there in midair.

"My god, it's some sort of anti-gravity field. You're actually producing a zero-g environment around yourself," Scott gasped.

"Mrrp!"

That must be how the dragon had slowed the Stargazer' fall. Somehow it had negated at least part of the Earth's gravitational pull over the ship. It hadn't been strong enough to stop the crash. Why was that? Because the field was too weak, or because it didn't extend far enough to cover most of the ship?

Scott dashed over to the medical computer and checked the scans his machine had made. He whistled. The machine was thorough, he'd give it that. Scott now had detailed anatomical data on dragons. That might prove incredibly helpful later on. Maybe they had a weakness he could learn and exploit.

But the wings — how did they work? He zoomed in on the analysis of the wing structures. There. At the ends of each bone, small structures that looked like the Hunter's organ on an electric eel.

"It's an electric charge," Scott said. "They're running an electric charge down through the wing material."

"Interesting. The electricity plus the unusual material of the bones running through the wings is generating a gravity field," Toby said, staring at the screen beside him.

"How did something like that evolve?" Scott breathed. "It's amazing."

"Different world, different evolution. If the dragons came here from that wandering planet, then they evolved under entirely different conditions from those on Earth," Toby replied.

"Better question is, what can we do with this information?" Scott asked.

"Mrrp!" Gorbash chirped, still hovering in the air next to him.

Scott turned at the sound and found himself nose-to-nose with the dragon. It leaned in and slurped his face with a long, wet tongue. He laughed, surprised. The critter was damned cute just fluttering there.

"I'm a little envious of you, Gorby," Scott said. "I wish I could get my ship aloft as easily as you can."

A thought struck like a thunderbolt. The dragon that died in the crash had almost been able to stop his ship's descent, even with all the velocity the Stargazer was still carrying. It's wing-field hadn't even reached most of the ship, from Scott's best guess.

That was a lot of power, and he had not one set of wing bones, but two. The Stargazer had no way to back itself out of the ground, but it had plenty of power from the reactor in the engine's core. All the electricity he could ask for.

"Toby, I've got a crazy idea," Scott said.

"This is news?"

Scott laughed. "I guess not. But this one is a doozy. Come on. I'm going to need your help. We've got a lot to do and not a ton of time."

If another attack arrived before he could put his plan into action, he'd have to find some way to fight them off. He might be able to do that, or he might not. The worst case was that the ship would end up damaged. That couldn't be allowed. The ship remained his best chance to escape this mess and survive.

"I'm going to climb up inside the ship toward the

engines," Scott said. "Your magnetic feet make it easier to get around on the outside of the hull."

He rummaged around in the storage locker. There had to be something in there he could use! The ship had damned near everything for just about any contingency. He could almost build a new Stargazer, given enough time. But time was the one thing he didn't have. It had to be a quick fix.

"You're making quite a mess," Toby said.

"Yeah, well, I need to find something," Scott said.

"If I knew what you were looking for, I might be able to help," Toby replied.

"I don't even know what I'm looking for," Scott said, sitting down with a sigh. "I want to attach the wing bones to the Stargazer. If I run a charge through them from the engines, it might be enough to get her airborne again."

"Would the hull sealant kits work?" Toby asked.

Scott blinked. That might just do the trick. They were packs of a resin that hardened almost as strong as the hull. He'd used one to quick-fix the meteor damage after the ship had taken a hit out in deep space. They still had plenty of the stuff on board.

"Go. Start clipping the bones to the hull. I'll run power conduits out through the airlock to link them up," Scott said.

"Not even a thank-you?" Toby asked, shaking his head.

"Thank you. Now get moving!" Scott laughed. He ran to the ladder and started climbing back toward the engines. It was going to take time to get all this done, and that was the one commodity they were short on.

Hooking up long wire leads to the reactor turned out to be the easy part. Toby had only finished gluing two bones to the hull by the time Scott had the leads hanging from the airlock. He wasn't thrilled about having to leave both airlock doors open for this to work, but there were no other holes for the cables. It left the ship vulnerable, but it would have to do until he could get a more permanent solution.

The ropes still hanging around the ship from Hector's work crews gave Scott the tools he needed to get the other bones up and into position. Four were glued to the lower hull. Those were relatively easy to put in place. The four he put around the aft section of the ship were a lot harder.

More than once, Scott found himself swallowing hard as he looked down. One slip, and he wouldn't be worried about finding the cure anymore. It put things into perspective for him in a way he hadn't felt in a long time.

Yeah, finding the cure was important. He wanted to live, damn it! But living was important, too. Scott had given up everything to find the cure. Now he was risking his life again to get the ship airborne and go looking for it again.

His resolve firmed up again. Nothing was going to stop him from getting to California. If the cure he needed was still out there somewhere, he was going to find it.

THIRTY-SEVEN

S cott stared up at the Stargazer from the ground, running his fingers through his hair. The ship had looked so elegant before. Now those clean lines were covered with wires and marred by bones stretching along the hull down much of the ship's length.

"It's a mess," Toby observed from beside him.

"It looks like something that ought to be flying the Jolly Roger," Scott agreed.

"Arrr."

Scott laughed. "Come on. Let's pump a little juice into those cables and see if this contraption actually works or not."

"Maybe just a little juice. We don't want to blow ourselves up," Toby said.

Scott climbed the ladder, privately agreeing with the robot. They knew next to nothing about the bone material or why it worked, just that it did. Take bone, add electricity, and you had a gravity field. It was like running power through tungsten and getting illumination. But wildly different, and outside every rule of physics he'd ever heard.

Working was good enough for now. He could figure out why later.

Scott reached the airlock door and was climbing inside when something pinged off the hull next to him. He glanced over and saw a spear rebounding from the metal. It fell to the ground. Another spear impacted a few feet below him.

"Shit!" Scott said, yanking his legs into the hatch. The treeline was a wall of people, all of them brandishing spears. None of them looked happy, and he couldn't close the hatch without cutting all the cables and undoing their work.

"Move it, Toby! Hostiles incoming!" Scott said. He darted inside, trusting the robot would follow close behind.

Scott all but dove down the accessway into the cockpit. There wasn't time to do testing, not now. The cameras showed the horde swarming from the trees, rushing across the open space straight at the Stargazer. Another few seconds and they'd be scaling the ladder. Scott patted the pistol he still had belted at his hip. He could fight off a few enemies, but not that many.

For a moment his hand hovered over the button that would close the hatch. That would lock them outside, but for how long? Eventually they'd bash their way in, and then he'd be back to trying to fight them all off again. It wasn't a winning proposition.

Instead, he picked up the little control panel he'd hacked together for the electrical cables. It had a long row of levers, each of which regulated the power going into one bone. The plan was to nudge the power up just a little to see what happened. There wasn't time for that anymore.

"Whatever you're doing, boss, I'd suggest you make it happen fast," Toby said. "They're climbing the ladder."

That settled things. He wasn't going to lose his ship today. No way.

Scott put his palm across the control box and shoved all of the levers up to the halfway position.

The ship shuddered. There was a creaking noise as the metal came under stress again. Scott winced with each new groan. The ship hadn't been built to handle strain of this sort, but she was a solid vessel. He was more worried about the resin holding the bones to the hull. If it came loose, the bones would go flying up and leave the ship behind — at least until they snapped free from the power lines.

There was another shake and the Stargazer began to slowly rise from the ground. It continued to climb at a steady rate. Within seconds, the ship was clearing the treetops.

"Yes!" Scott said. He boosted the power to the nose-mounted bones, and the nose of the ship swung upward.

Once they were leveled out, he decreased the power across the board to about twenty-five percent. That seemed about right to keep them level, floating a few hundred feet above the trees.

"Company coming!" Toby warned.

Scott whirled back toward the open hatch just as the first snarling warrior came inside. He stood from the pilot's chair and yanked his pistol from its holster.

At this point shooting was becoming second nature to him. His attacker took a few steps toward him before Scott pulled the trigger three times, putting him down for good.

"How many?" Scott called.

"Camera says one more in the airlock, one more outside. These guys are persistent!"

That was one word for it. Crazy might be the other. Scott couldn't imagine clinging to the outside of a ship as it started taking off. What if he'd been taking the ship into orbit?

Of course, these people had no concept of flight aside from dragons. Scott still wondered at the courage of people who clung to the ship as it shot upward. He shook his head. It was a damned shame to have to fight people like that, but he doubted he was going to convince them to give up.

The second warrior came in through the inner door as he was thinking. Scott raised the pistol again and fired. The shot blasted the man backward into the airlock. He crawled backward. Scott frowned and shook his head.

"I'm not being stopped today. Not by you or anyone else."

He fired again. The shot sent the man tumbling out the hatch into open air.

"Where's the third one, Toby?" Scott asked.

"Still outside on the ladder. Looks like he's messing with the cables."

That was no good. Lose the power from those cables and the ship would fall. Just as he had the thought, the ship shuddered and leaned to one side, slipping slowly toward the treetops.

"He cut one, boss! Better stop him. He's working on another," Toby said.

"Boost power five percent to the other bones to compensate," Scott called out.

Then he went forward into the airlock. Wind whistled through the opening as the ship continued to tilt and drift. Scott held on to rails as the ground swung by beneath his view for a moment. The trees were still coming closer, but it was a long way down.

He grabbed onto a rail with his left hand, holding the pistol in his right, and leaned outside the hatch. The man was there, hanging on the ladder. But his legs were sticking out straight away from the ship, like gravity was sideways! He was near one of the bones. It had to be warping gravity around him enough to leave him hanging like that.

In the man's hand was a steel knife. He was working to get close enough to another cable to slice through it.

"Don't do it!" Scott shouted, struggling to be heard over the howling wind.

He didn't want to shoot, damn it. Anyone with as much guts as this man showed was someone who shouldn't die like this. But he wasn't going to allow him to crash the ship, either.

The man glanced up at him, his face a mixture of terror and fury. He must have seen the gun in Scott's hand, but probably had no idea what it was. He grabbed the nearest cable and brought the knife up to slice through it.

Scott pulled the trigger.

The bullet slammed into the warrior. His mouth opened in a startled O, and then he shot sideways away from the Stargazer about a hundred yards before arcing toward the ground. A moment later he was gone, vanished into the treetops.

Scott hauled himself back inside the ship and holstered the pistol. His hands felt dirty, unclean from all the blood they'd spilled today. He'd gone from being a man who'd never killed anyone to someone who pulled the trigger without more than a second's hesitation.

That he'd been forced to do those things because of the nature of the world he'd found himself in didn't make it feel any better. But at least it was done now. The Stargazer was airborne. He could put all of this behind him.

Scott settled into the pilot's seat once more and powered up the laser drive.

"It's time to head west, Toby. We've been off track too long," he said.

He flicked another switch and the drive lit up, sending a high powered beam stabbing out from behind the vessel. The laser was heavily attenuated by the air it passed through, only stabbing back a thousand meters or so before losing power. But it was hot enough to superheat the air it came in contact with. The expanding air behind the ship created a pressure wave that sent the Stargazer forward.

Angling the laser let Scott steer the ship. The switches on his new control panel would let him adjust altitude. Finally, he had the power to get underway. He turned the ship's nose toward sunset and added a little more power to the laser, shooting the ship forward.

THIRTY-EIGHT

Scott kept their speed down. He didn't know how the rough patches attaching the bones would react to high speed, so it seemed the safest course. The last thing he needed was to have bones start falling off when they were moving a few hundred miles an hour.

Toby had already patched the damaged line, but the ease with which that guy had sliced through it just emphasized how vulnerable this quick-fix really was. He'd need to make more permanent modifications as soon as it was safe to land.

A cruising speed of twenty miles an hour was enough to get them out of the immediate area, anyway. Once they were clear of this little war they'd found themselves in the middle of, Scott could worry about finding a place to set the ship down.

He kept the Stargazer close to the treetops, too. Two dragons was more than enough. If he poured on the speed, he could probably outrun any dragon that saw them and attacked, but then he ran a risk of wrecking the ship. Better to drift along and avoid attention.

"That's smoke," Toby said, breaking into his thoughts.

They'd only traveled a couple of miles. The smoke was rising through trees another four or five miles away. There was a lot of it, too. More thick black smoke was coming up by the minute.

"It's Hero's Keep, isn't it," Scott said. "That's where Tamara and Hector live."

"The coordinates look about right. I'd guess the battle isn't going well for them," Toby said, his voice solemn.

"Not our problem," Scott said, slicing his hand across the air in front of him to emphasize his words. "We have a rendezvous with the west coast, and we're overdue."

Toby didn't reply, leaving Scott alone to his thoughts. The ship continued forward, the tall plume of smoke gradually coming nearer until they passed by about two miles north of it. Scott trained a rear-mounted camera on the pillar as the Stargazer cruised on.

He wondered how Tamara was doing down there. Was she fighting for her life, trying to defend those long tunnels? What would happen to the rest of those people, if the warriors fell and their enemies took the Keep? This was a harsh world. Scott had a feeling the penalty for losing was equally dire.

They'd hit him over the head and taken him prisoner, then tried to capture his ship. It wasn't like he owed Hector anything. But then, Tamara had rescued him. Or tried to, anyway. She'd done her best to right her father's wrongs.

Hector wasn't a bad sort in his own way, either. He was a product of his environment. Scott couldn't imagine what it was like, trying to maintain a population in a barbaric world where dragons ruled the skies. He'd been trying to do the best he could for his people. When Scott helped rescue

Tamara from the dragon, Hector had stepped up and offered to return the favor.

He had honor. That was more than Scott could say about most of the people he knew back in the twenty-first century.

It made him wonder if leaving those people to their fate was the honorable thing to do. He realized it probably wasn't, but damn it, he had to get going, or he was going to run out of time! It was sheer luck he'd even been able to get the Stargazer back in the air, and there was no telling how long he'd be able to keep her there.

"Shit. Shit, shitty, shittiest," Scott growled.

He yanked on the controls, firing the nose thrusters to spin the ship rapidly around. In only a short time, he had the nose aimed back toward the smoke plume.

"We going back?" Toby asked.

"Yeah."

"What's the plan?"

"We're going to go kick a little ass, rescue Hector and Tamara from the mess they're in. Then we're headed out west," Scott said, and he meant it.

Maybe he couldn't leave these people to their fate, but his own would be sealed if he didn't see to his future soon.

Scott brought down the laser's power level as they drew closer. By the time they were over the little clearing in front of the Keep, the Stargazer was almost stationary. The battle raging below them had largely stopped, too. Everyone was too busy staring at the sky, trying to figure out what they were looking at.

The ship wasn't a dragon, so most of the people below weren't dashing away in fear. Tamara would recognize the ship, though. Scott just hoped she would be able to rally her people enough to take advantage of the confusion he was sowing.

"Hold our position above the clearing," Scott told Toby.

"Got it. Where are you going?"

"They're afraid of dragons, but not of the Stargazer? It's time to show them why they should be."

He stopped by the weapons locker and snatched the AR-15 back up, grabbing a vest full of magazines at the same time. Reloads were going to end up being an issue before too long if he had to keep using rounds like this. But while he had the guns, they represented an insurmountable advantage for his team. Scott figured he should take any edge he could get.

The breeze blew only lightly through the open airlock doors. Scott smelled the smoke wafting in with the wind. One side or both had used fire as an attack, and there were bits of still-burning material scattered all over the battleground.

He leaned out, scanning the field. The attackers had hauled up several large constructs on wheels. They were trying to pull those towers up to the edge of the wall so they could climb in through the top. So far, they hadn't succeeded, but one tower was coming close.

The men and women hauling the tower were shielded from Hector's people attacking them. But the cover's angle didn't give them any shelter from Scott's weapon. He took aim with the rifle and fired a shot.

It pinged off a wheel.

The target was too far away to make aiming easy. He lay down on the floor of the airlock, bracing the rifle as carefully as he could, and squeezed the trigger again. This time, one of the attackers went down. He shifted his aim point and fired again. Another fallen foe.

Now the others were looking around, alarmed. The tower's forward motion ceased. That would do for the moment. Scott swept the barrel across the field, looking for anything that resembled a command post.

There! That clump of warriors all together in a circle. The people in the middle of the cluster would probably be important. Scott squeezed off a shot at one of them, but missed and hit a guard from the circle instead.

The rest of the circle froze for only a second when they saw their fellow guard drop. Then they closed ranks, drawing heavy shields over their heads and obscuring the people in the middle from view.

"We're too high! Bring us down to about fifty feet!" Scott hollered over his shoulder.

The ship lurched and began descending. Closer to the targets was a good thing. Scott began opening up on clumps of attackers, firing as rapidly as the AR-15 would allow. He figured even if half his shots missed, the raw terror he was spreading in the enemy ranks was enough to disrupt their attack.

A horn sounded, and the main gates of Hero's Keep opened up. Scott grinned. Tamara, taking her cue! He spotted her at the vanguard of the force exiting, spear and shield in her hands. With a roar, her people rushed forward, forming a wedge as they advanced into the enemy ranks.

They were still grossly outnumbered, but Scott continued pouring fire into the attacking force. The rear of the enemy formations was breaking. He watched as one warrior after another fled the line and ran back into the trees. Caught between the crush of the Keep fighters and Scott's brutal firepower, many chose to flee.

"Radar contact!" Toby said into the radio in Scott's ear.

"Radar contact? What could be showing up on radar?" Scott asked a moment before realizing what it had to be.

A deafening roar drowned out all other noise as the dragon banked, winging in over the clearing.

THIRTY-NINE

S cott was moving while echoes of the roar still reverberated around the ship. He all but flew into the cockpit and hit the controls, pouring more electricity into the wing bones. The Stargazer shot skyward, rising so rapidly it took the wind out of his lungs.

Just below the cloud level, Scott slowed their ascent and checked the cameras. The dragon was circling the clearing but still glancing up at the ship.

"Like it's not sure whether to go after us, or stick around and eat them," Scott said.

"It looks like the battle is over," Toby observed. "The attackers are fleeing into the forest, and Tamara's people are returning to the Keep."

The ship must have been far enough away that the dragon felt safe. It stooped and landed on top of the massive walls blocking the tunnel entrance. Reaching down with its mouth, it tried getting inside the hole to the tunnels below, but it couldn't fit more than the tip of its snout. Scott heaved a sigh of relief. It looked like her people would be safe in there.

Then the dragon raked the rocks with its claws. The shaking of the wall was so great that it was visible even from Scott's altitude. One rock tumbled away from the rest, crashing to the ground. The dragon started clawing away at a second stone.

"It's breaking in," Scott said.

"It would seem so."

"All those people!" There had to be something he could do.

"We don't have any weapon systems on the Stargazer capable of killing a dragon," Toby warned. "Your heavy rifle might do the trick again, but probably not before it did critical damage to the bones holding us aloft."

"We've got to try," Scott said. He brought the nose of the ship down and then reduced power to the bones. Their altitude dropped in a rush, the dragon seeming to race toward them as the ship dove toward the ground.

Scot activated the ship's external speakers. "Hey, ugly! Come and pick on someone bigger than you!"

The dragon looked up. Startled by the ship's sudden reappearance and rapid descent, the dragon launched itself into the air. Its wings glowed brightly as it went airborne, hissing anger.

Scott slowed their drop, coming about level with the furious lizard. "You've got the controls, Toby. Get me in line for a good shot."

"I'll do my best," Toby said.

The AR wasn't going to do more than make this thing mad. Toby was right. His best shot was the big bore rifle. He grabbed the weapon and slapped a magazine in on his way back to the airlock, grabbing a spare magazine and stuffing it into his pocket. Toby started spinning the ship, bringing the dragon into his view. Scott took aim and fired.

The shot hit the dragon somewhere in the chest. It roared, hurt but not out of the fight. Now it knew the ship could hurt it. The dragon wasn't willing to back down from a fight, but it wasn't going to float there and let him take potshots at it, either.

The creature darted forward. Two heavy wingbeats carried it the distance to the Stargazer. Claws sank into the metal hull with a scream of tearing steel. Two of the cables powering the bones were cut, and the ship tilted wildly to one side.

Scott didn't have time for more than a yelp as the ship tilted. One moment he was looking out the side, the next the airlock door was aimed straight at the ground. He tumbled out, losing his grip on the rifle. Something snaked past his shoulder as he fell, and Scott grabbed for it.

The cable burned his fingers with friction as he slid down it, braking his fall. He was alive! The ground was dizzyingly far below, and he was ten feet down from the ship, hanging by an electrical cable, but he was alive.

Maybe not for long, though. The dragon saw him falling and craned its neck to watch his progress. As Scott swung back and forth on the end of the cable, the dragon's head tracked his movement like a kitten watching the end of a piece of string. Scott swallowed hard. The dragon bunched its hindquarters and launched itself into the air again.

Before it could snap him into its mouth, something small and fast darted past Scott. The rush of air from its passage almost made him let go of the cable again, but he clung to it for all he was worth.

"MRRP!"

It was Gorbash! Scott watched as the small dragonet swooped in so he was nose to nose with the bigger dragon. He made a long series of angry chirping noises at it.

The big dragon opened its mouth and roared back, hard enough that the wind from its breath sent Gorbash back several feet. But the baby dragon had game, Scott had to hand him that much. He fluttered back closer and gave his best roar in return.

It wasn't all that loud. Scott could imagine the bigger dragon chuckling to itself. It reached out a claw and swatted at Gorbash. The dragonet dove under the swing and came up again hissing. When the big dragon slid sideways to go around Gorbash, he moved with it, carefully keeping himself between the big beastie and Scott.

"He's protecting me," Scott said. "But he's gonna get killed. Toby, we have to help Gorbash."

"What do you have in mind, boss?" Toby replied over the radio.

"Power up the laser. Activate the bow thrusters and spin the ship on my mark."

"On it," Toby replied.

Scott returned his attention to the dragon. It was growing more frustrated, and took another swing at Gorbash. The little dragon dodged again, but the big one came in with a second claw strike too rapidly for him to avoid it. The claw slammed into Gorbash, sending him spinning away.

There was nothing between the big dragon and Scott, now. He swallowed hard. The dragon swept back its wings and opened its mouth wide.

"Now, Toby!"

The bow thrusters screamed into life, spinning the ship hard around. The Stargazer's bow pivoted sharply away from the dragon.

Then the laser drive cut on.

A bright beam lashed out from the rear of the Stargazer.

The laser superheated the air around it for a short, three-second burst as the ship continued its spin.

The dragon didn't even have time to roar. As the ship spun, the beam cut through the air where it hovered. It was hot enough to instantly combust almost anything it touched. The beam cut through flesh and bone as easily as air, slicing the dragon in half.

Burning fragments of the creature crashed to the ground, shaking the trees for half a mile around.

Scott heaved a sigh of relief. With shaking hands, he tried to climb back up the cable, but realized he was never going to make it back up.

"Awesome work, Toby. Now, can you lower me down before I fall off this thing?" Scott called out.

"I have to do everything around here," the robot replied.

Scott opened his mouth to make a retort, but couldn't. He was too busy laughing. It came out as a chuckle at first, but quickly turned into a deep belly laugh that continued even after his feet were safely on the ground again.

FORTY

Scott ordered Toby to take the ship aloft again as soon as he was safely down. While he was fairly sure most of the enemy force had fled, there was no telling whether they'd return now that the dragon was dead. He had to keep the Stargazer out of their hands at any cost.

Especially now that they'd seen him use the main drive as a weapon. It didn't matter that the laser had never been intended to function that way. The people watching him use it to kill another dragon weren't going to see it that way. All they knew was that he'd killed another of the creatures.

Gorbash seemed OK, at least. The dragonet fluttered his way back into the airlock. Scott figured he was probably already rummaging about for a snack. He shook his head in wonder. The little dragon had saved his life, going up against a much bigger creature to keep it from killing him.

Somewhere on the ground was his rifle. He wasn't sure it had survived the fall, but even broken, it might be dangerous for the same reason any other tech could be. These people were lacking in knowledge about technology, but they weren't stupid.

He scanned the ground where the weapon ought to be, searching for the gleam of metal that would reveal it, but there was no sign. Had it fallen elsewhere? Was he wrong about where it had dropped? Scott didn't think so, and a chill went down his back at the thought someone might have picked the weapon up.

Before he could do anything to continue the search, he heard someone calling his name. Scott looked up to see Tamara racing toward him.

"Scott! Please come quickly," she said, out of breath as she came up alongside him.

"What's wrong?" Scott asked, his hand flowing toward the pistol at his side like it was second nature now. That it was now so easy for him to respond to a potential threat with violence felt both relieving and disturbing at the same time.

"It's my father. He needs you. Please come quickly!"

Scott simply nodded, sensing time was of the essence. Tamara took off again, racing back toward the keep. He followed close behind, finding his way through the twisted ruins left behind by the battle. It would be a long time before the ground here returned to the way he'd first seen it. Now the rocks were slick with the blood of the fallen.

They passed by the still-steaming corpse of the dragon. Scott gave it only a passing glance. He'd killed three of the things now. How many more of them were there? Even after he found his cure, the dragons were going to remain a problem he had to solve.

It was one he could deal with later, though. Tamara slowed as she approached a knot of people gathered in front of the Keep's door. That had to be where Hector was, which meant he hadn't been inside resting like he ought to have been. He must have joined his people in the rush to rout their enemies.

Damn the man. He wasn't in any shape for a fight like that. Those wounds he had taken earlier might not have been immediately fatal, but they were bad enough. He needed rest if he was going to have any chance of recovery.

"Toby, warm up the medical pod. Hector is hurt. I think we may need a quick evac and treatment for him," Scott said over his radio link.

"On it. I'll bring the ship closer and prepare to descend."

The people parted as Tamara stepped forward. She knelt beside a bloody ruin of a body. Scott sucked in a breath as he drew close enough to see the person's face.

It was Hector.

He was horribly injured. The old wounds had come open again, and he had brand new ones as well. Multiple arrows sprouted from his chest and abdomen. Deep slashes marred all of his limbs. Scott couldn't understand how the man was still alive, but he for sure wouldn't be for very long.

"Toby, step on it," Scott said. He came in close and knelt beside Tamara. "Hang in there. We're going to get you into my medical bay. Get you patched right up."

He hoped it could do the job. The auto-doc was incredibly capable, but it had limits. Scott had a bad feeling that injuries this extensive might be too much even for his technology. That didn't matter, though. He had to try.

"Help me get him up," Scott said to the people watching. He slipped his arms beneath Hector, intending to lift him. But Hector screamed a hoarse cry at the smallest movement.

Scott withdrew his arms. They were soaked with blood.

He shook his head, trying to figure out what to do. There had to be a way.

But Hector shook his head, his face sad. He beckoned with the fingers of one hand, no strength left for much more than that. Scott, Tamara, and many of the onlookers leaned in close to hear his words.

"I appreciate you trying, my friend. But is it too late for me, even with all your wonders?" Hector said.

Scott nodded slowly. He felt his eyes growing moist.

"I thought as much. Tamara will be chief after I am gone," Hector said, putting enough volume into his words that all around could hear his wishes.

"I am not ready, father," she said.

"You are. But you will need help. Our people face potential extermination. Four tribes have rallied to fight us. They are gone," Hector said, coughing red. "But not for long. The Keep wall is damaged, and even with it, holding out would be hard."

Scott had a feeling he knew what was coming next. Part of him wanted to run away, to flee now, before the man could ask of him something he couldn't give. But he held his ground. Hector had earned that much from him.

"You, my young friend. You have the power to help my daughter save our people, Scott. Will you stand by her?" Hector asked. "I know you have your own quest, but will you stay until the threat is past and my people are safe?"

He wanted to say no, to fly away and not look back even for a moment. But the desperation he saw in the dying man's eyes was too much. Hector was passing. Nothing Scott could do would alter that, he sensed that even as he glanced over his shoulder to see how close the Stargazer was to the ground.

There was no saving Hector, but maybe Scott could send him on with hope for his people, instead of fear.

"I will stay and help your people grow strong again, Hector," Scott said.

"Thank you," Hector replied, smiling at last. He reached out an arm and clasped Scott's forearm to his own.

Then Hector looked skyward. "I am sorry I cannot stay, my daughter. I love you."

Tamara leaned in to hold her father, crying silent tears on his shoulder. "I know. I love you too. I will do everything I can to be a chief like you."

"Be better than me, Tamara. You have it in you," Hector said.

There was a crunching noise as the Stargazer set down. Scott looked up and saw Toby standing in the open airlock.

"Medical bay is ready!" Toby cried.

Scott whirled back to the chief, but he'd stopped breathing. He was already gone. Was there still a chance the pod could pull him back? The blood pooled around the man said otherwise.

"Help me lift him," Scott said, scooping his arms under the chief's body again. At first no one moved, so he added "Right now!"

Several people helped Scott lift Hector's body. With him guiding them, they brought their chief into the Stargazer and lay him down in the pod. Scott tapped commands and the lid slipped shut. Immediately the medical unit began assessing the patient. An IV was started, fluids inserted. Pads lifted to Hector's chest and Scott winced as the patient's body shook from defibrillation.

"What is it doing?" Tamara asked.

"Trying to save him. Sometimes, there is time even after

the last breath, before life fully leaves the body," Scott explained.

"Magic?" breathed one of the tribesmen.

"Technology," Scott replied. "Science. Your damned birthright, before it was stolen from you."

He was angrier than he'd been in a long time. There should be hospitals with the technology to help heal this man. Hell, there should be better tech than he'd ever imagined by this year. Instead, he was back in caveman days, for all intents and purposes.

The pod shocked Hector a third time. This time, it got a small but steady heartbeat.

"Yes! He's back," Scott said.

"Alive?" Tamara asked.

"Alive. But he's got a long way to go," Scott replied, watching as the device continued to patch up the chief and work on his extensive injuries while struggling to keep him breathing and his heart beating. "He'll be asleep for days, maybe longer."

"But he will live," Tamara breathed.

"If he stays strong, yes. It's not a guarantee, but I'll do all I can for him, I promise," Scott said.

"Will you still stay?" she asked, looking away from her father and up at Scott.

"Of course. I told Hector I would. That still holds. I'll help you protect your people until this crisis is over," Scott said.

Saying those words brought Scott mixed emotions. He felt fear for his own future and loss for the quest he had to abandon, at least for now.

But he also felt good about himself. Better than he had in a long time, actually. All of the work to get the Stargazer built had been for himself. Surviving in deep space had been about him.

Now he was acting for others, and Scott realized he liked that feeling.

FORTY-ONE

Later that day, Scott rested in the pilot's chair, staring down at the people working below. He had a lot of work to do, too. But it had been one hell of a last couple of days. The work could begin tomorrow.

For this evening and tonight, Scott intended to rest as best he could. Radar would warn him of incoming dragons, and floating fifty feet off the ground should keep him out of reach of everyone else. It also ought to scare away any war parties who thought now might be a good time to attack again.

They wouldn't remain cowed forever. Hector had been right, they'd come back. Scott intended to make sure the people below were ready when they did.

"Hector is still in a medical coma," Toby said, stepping back into the cockpit. "No real change."

"Thanks for checking on him," Scott replied.

It would be touch and go for a while yet. The days ahead would determine if Hector would live or die. Scott hoped the man would make it. He was gambling with a lot of medical supplies that he would survive. But then, it just wasn't in Scott to give up on anything without a fight.

"We're really staying then, boss?" Toby asked in a quiet voice.

Scott looked over at him. "We are. I promised Hector we'd keep his people safe, at least for now."

"What about your cure?" Toby asked.

Surprising himself, Scott laughed. He thought he was still broken up about not flying west right away, but he felt lighter than ever.

"Toby, that cure might not even be out there. But if it is, it's waited two hundred years. It'll probably survive a little longer," Scott said. "These people, though? We might be their last shot at having anything better than this."

How many humans were left on Earth, all scattered in small and isolated bands like this? It didn't look like they were thriving or growing. Seemed more like they were feeding off the remnants of the old world, using up whatever resources were available.

Scott's technology might be the last high-tech equipment still functioning on Earth. If there was ever going to be a shot at humanity coming back to be more than what he saw right now, he was going to have to do the heavy lifting.

"We might be the last hope humanity has of ever getting out of this dark age. Maybe of even surviving at all," Scott whispered. The words felt like they had a weight of their own, settling over his shoulders.

"In that case, I have been instructed to play a message for you," Toby said. He sat down next to Scott, and suddenly his voice changed to another one Scott knew almost as well as his own. It was his mother speaking.

"Scott, if you're hearing this then the shit has truly hit the fan," his mother's recording began. "But if Toby is playing this for you, it also means you've decided to do something about it."

How could she have known something would be wrong with Earth? Scott gaped, trying to consider all the implications.

"What did you do, mom?" he whispered. She didn't reply; it truly was just a recording.

"We've known a rogue planet was on the way for a long time now. It's due to come near Earth sometime after you depart. I probably won't be around to see it, but you might have been. It's probably going to screw things up badly. Big old fashioned apocalypse. I wasn't sure what you'd find upon returning, so I helped make sure the Stargazer was packed with anything you might need for any eventuality."

"Betcha didn't expect dragons," Scott said with a small smile.

"Toby is only going to play this if you decide to put the needs of others ahead of your own. In which case, I'm damned proud of you, son," his mother said. "I wish I could be there to help, but since I can't, I sent them the next best thing: my brilliant child."

"I don't know what you found when you arrived," she went on. "I can't predict what will happen when the planet passes Earth. Just that it won't be good. Whatever you've run into so far might not be the worst you'll see, either. But as you've probably already figured out, you may be the last shot human beings have at rising out of whatever ashes are left when you get there."

Scott leaned back in his seat. The tears he'd barely managed to hold back for Hector tumbled down his cheeks now. Hearing his mother's voice from all those centuries ago undid all the self-control he had left.

"One last thing. Toby has coordinates for a supply

cache I am setting up. I'm putting it someplace geologically stable and digging it in deep enough that it should survive whatever comes. It's the best I can offer you. No promises, but I'd recommend going there when you can to see what's left," she said. "I'm proud of you, Scott. You never thought you were worth much, and that made me sad. But you've always been smarter and stronger than you thought. There's a lot riding on your shoulders out there in the future. But I have faith you can make it happen. Good luck."

Then Toby's voice went back to normal. "End of recording."

When Scott was able to stop crying, he looked up at Toby. "Are there more like that? More voice recordings she left for me?"

"I didn't know that one was there until you triggered it. If there are more, they're buried by a trigger, too," Toby said. "I do have those coordinates she mentioned, though. It's a spot about three hundred miles north of here. We gonna go?"

"Not right away," Scott said. "Too risky to leave everyone this vulnerable. But yeah, we'll go check it out as soon as we can."

Scott leaned back in his chair again, watching the moon rise over the towering trees. His mother had faith in him. Hell, she'd always believed in him, apparently. She was the smartest person he'd ever known. If she thought he could do something about the mess Earth was in, well, he'd just have to work at it until he managed.

"Scott Free, Dragonslayer. Has a nice ring to it, doesn't it?" he asked Toby.

"Mrrp!" Gorbash said, fluttering over and depositing himself in Scott's lap.

"Not of you, oh flying hot dog eater!" Scott laughed. "You get to stick with us."

Gorbash slurped his face with a long tongue, then curled up under his arm and went to sleep.

Rest came slowly for Scott. His mind was busy with plans about what he would do the following day. But that was for then. Eventually he let his eyelids close, and he dreamed of dragons and starlight.

AUTHOR'S NOTES

This story was a ton of fun to write. I hope you enjoyed reading it as much as I did penning the words! If the story is popular with readers, I have in mind several more tales involving Scott and Toby.

"The Quantum Dragonslayer" has an interesting origin story. Back in the summer of 2018, there was a brief kerfuffle in the writing world around trademarks. Several authors began trademarking common words and issuing takedown notices on books which used those words.

Now, I've got no issues with intellectual property. As a writer, that's how I make my living: I make up things that people value enough to pay me for them. (Thank you, by the way!)

But two of the words being trademarked were problematic for a lot of science fiction and fantasy authors: 'quantum' and 'dragonslayer'. SFWA (The Science Fiction and Fantasy Writers of America) got involved in the legal dispute, and as a member I encouraged their participation. Then another member suggested I get some skin in the game by writing a story using the proposed trademarks SFWA was fighting.

It took me all of a day of brainstorming to come up with a fun, lively, interesting, exciting idea that used both quantum and dragonslayer at the same time.

However, the whole thing got resolved amicably long before the book was finished! That left me with a good story that didn't really have a deep purpose anymore.

But it was still a good story. It went out to my editor, and came back.

I spent some time cleaning the work up, making it a little better as the months went by. I wanted this book to be light; not comedy, but fun and sort of breezy in tone. Some of my work feels incredibly serious. This was an attempt to do something a bit different.

Then it was sent out to my advanced reader team, some of whom sent me back a whole swath of last typos. Especially helpful was Norma Grogan, whose keen eye found more typos than anyone else! Also special thanks to Mark Frink, whose keen eye was invaluable.

It was a fun voyage, bringing Scott and Toby to you. I hope I've done well with it.

If you loved this book, drop a review on Amazon? How readers react to this first novel will tell me whether it's a winner worth pursuing or not.

Feel free to write to me with your thoughts as well! I can be reached at kevins.studio@gmail.com, and love hearing from readers!

Thanks again for reading. You make everything possible.

Kevin

OTHER BOOKS BY KEVIN
MCLAUGHLIN

Book 3 - Accord of Valor
Book 4 - Ghost Wing
Book 5 - Ghost Squadron
Book 6 - Ghost Fleet (2019)

Valhalla Online Series (A Ragnarok Saga Story)
Book 1 - Valhalla Online
Book 2 - Raiding Jotunheim
Book 3 - Vengeance Over Vanaheim
Book 4 - Hel Hath No Fury

**Lost Planet Warriors (Military SF with light
romance)**
Book 1 - Desperate Times
Book 2 - Desperate Measures
Dire Straits - Free short story for email list
fans!

Blackwell Magic Series (Urban Fantasy)
Book 1 - By Darkness Revealed
Book 2 - Ashes Ascendant
Book 3 - Dead In Winter
Book 4 - Claws That Catch
Book 5 - Darkness Awakes
Book 6 - Spellbinding Entanglements
By A Whisker (short story)
The Raven and the Rose - Free novelette for
email list fans!

Dead Brittania Series:
Dead Brittania (short prequel story)
Book 1 - King of the Dead
Book 2 - Queen of Demons

Raven's Heart Series (Urban Fantasy)
Book 1 - Stolen Light
Book 2 - Webs in the Dark
Book 3 - Shades of Moonlight

Other Titles:
Over the Moon (SF romance)
Midnight Visitors (Steampunk Cat short story)
Demon Ex Machina (Steampunk Cat short story)
The Coffee Break Novelist (help for writers!)
You Must Write (Heinlein's rules for writers)

KEVIN MCLAUGHLIN

ACCORD OF
FIRE

Exclusive for fans of the Accord series!
Find out how the story started... When Captain Nicholas
Stein set out to stop one enemy ship, and set in motion
events which shaped the course of human history for
decades to come.
http://kevinomclaughlin.com/accordoffire/

ABOUT THE AUTHOR

USA Today bestselling author Kevin McLaughlin has written more than three dozen science fiction and fantasy novels, along with more short stories than he can easily count. Kevin can be found most days in downtown Boston, working on the next novel. His bestselling Blackwell Magic fantasy series, Accord science fiction series, Valhalla Online LitRPG series, and the fan-favorite Starship Satori series are ongoing.

I love hearing from readers!

www.kevinomclaughlin.com
kevins.studio@gmail.com

.

Manufactured by Amazon.ca
Bolton, ON

11140402R00148